Outlaw Ambush!

Calmly, working by feel, he continued feeding shells into the Winchester's magazine, his fingers moving with the speed and precision born of long experience.

While he was working, Longarm had kept his eyes on Smith. When he saw the outlaw's hands stop shaking and raise one of his revolvers, Longarm was sliding the last cartridge into the Winchester's loading-port. He levered a shell into the chamber, took quick aim, and fired. The slug smashed into Smith's ribcage as the outlaw triggered his revolver.

Echoes of both Smith's and Longarm's shots were dying in the air when a rifle barked behind Longarm and the slug whistled past his ear. As he was turning his head to look for the man who'd apparently out-flanked him, the rifle cracked again. This time the bullet lifted Longarm's hat off his head.

Even before his hat started falling to earth, Longarm was rolling over to bring his rifle to bear on the outlaw who was sniping at him from behind. What he saw almost froze his finger on the Winchester's trigger...

— TABOR EVANS —

LONGARM

ON DEADMAN'S TRAIL

J

JOVE BOOKS, NEW YORK

LONGARM ON DEADMAN'S TRAIL

A Jove Book/published by arrangement with
the author

PRINTING HISTORY
Jove edition/October 1987

ISBN: 0-515-09215-0

Chapter 1

As soft as the sound was, a faint tinkle of rain pattering on the windows of his room broke through Longarm's sleep. He sat up in bed, glancing toward the shaded windows. Gray light, the subdued glimmer of a cloudy sky, showed through the tattered shades. Though the room itself was still dim, Longarm needed no light at all to step from the bed to the windows and pull the shade aside. He saw just what he'd expected to see: a lead-gray sky from which spatters of drops were falling, flattening into wet blobs on the window panes and trickling down to the sill.

Well, old son, he told himself silently as he let the shade drop to shield his eyes from the unwelcome sight. *rain's bad enough, but at least it ain't snow. And it ain't likely to be, what with summer coming on real fast. Maybe it'll clear up by the time you get dressed and start for the office.*

There were cigars and matches lying beside the bottle of Tom Moore on the battered oak dresser, and Longarm lighted one of his long slim cheroots before picking up the bottle of

1

Maryland rye. A puff of the cheroot followed by a healthy swallow of the pungent whiskey failed to improve his sagging spirits, but a second swallow and another deep drag on the cigar got him out of the doldrums that always plagued him when rain or snow greeted him on wakening.

As he put the bottle back on the dresser, the neat round holes in the crimped-in crown of his snuff-brown Stetson caught his eye. He picked up the hat and with his other hand inside the crown, slid a finger into each of the holes. Wriggling the tips of the protruding fingers, Longarm shook his head thoughtfully while his thumb moved along the edge of the hat's wide brim, feeling the rounded nick that his quarry's second shot had cut.

That's another time when you had an angel setting on your shoulder, he told himself. *If either one of them slugs had landed about an inch lower, you wouldn't be standing here looking at them raindrops. You'd be laying stretched out in a pine box under six feet of dirt, and it wouldn't make no nevermind whether it was raining or snowing or the sun was shining. That damn Charlie Batson was a better shot than you gave him credit for being.*

For more than a week Longarm had trailed Batson. His chase had begun deep in Dakota Territory, where he'd picked up the escaped murderer's trail in the little village of Belle Fourche, close to the Wyoming line. His quarry had proved to be both fast-moving and shrewd about zigzagging through the edge of the Black Hills. In that rugged country, Longarm had lost the trail several times, but circling the area had always allowed him to pick it up again. Then, after crossing Cold Brook and entering another corner of the Dakota's badlands, Batson's skill in hiding his track seemed to have deserted him, and he'd left a trail a child could have followed.

For a skilled tracker such as Longarm, the fugitive's progress was so plain that he could almost have done the last forty miles of his tracking while blindfolded. Then Batson had taken refuge in the decrepit barn of a homestead that long ago had been abandoned by a discouraged farmer. There was the skeleton of a house standing some distance away from the barn, but no other cover of any sort.

2

On all sides of the decaying buildings the farmer had cleared the land in a futile effort to raise row crops. Longarm had seen dozens of such farms everywhere in the West. They represented the ends of dreams of Eastern farmers too stubborn to listen to the warnings of earlier emigrants who'd tried to convince them that cattle were the only crops anyone could figure on harvesting from a land grant in Dakota Territory.

Through the wide cracks between the warped boards of the barn's deteriorating walls, Longarm could get occasional glimpses of both Batson and his horse. The horse's form was outlined clearly, a dark shape seen through the inch-wide gaps separating the wide boards. Batson was less highly visible, but Longarm could occasionally see his form outlined, too.

Taking the only choice he saw, Longarm had spurred his horse to the framework which was all that remained of the farmhouse. The long-abandoned building was little more than studding and foundation timbers. It would provide scanty cover, but was a better choice than the barren prairie which stretched baldly in all directions to the horizon.

A few wide foundation timbers still spanned the bottom of the house-skeleton. Longarm grabbed the stock of his Winchester and yanked it from its saddle-scabbard as he dived to the ground, regained his balance after a momentary stumble, then bent over and ran into what was left of the dwelling. He dived behind the foundation timbers just as the crack of Batson's first shot broke the still air and the rifle's slug kicked up dust inches away from the marks in the dust Longarm's feet had left when he'd dived for cover.

There were cracks between the foundation timbers, but none of them were wide enough to allow Longarm to slide the barrel of his Winchester between them, and he had no notion of raising his head above them. Even the few seconds that would be required for him to shoulder and aim the Winchester would mean offering himself to Batson as a clear target. Peering through the cracks, Longarm could glimpse the outlaw killer's silhouette in the barn, outlined in the wide gaps between its vertical boards.

"You might as well give up, Batson!" Longarm called. He raised his head as he spoke. "I don't cotton much to digging you a grave out here on the prairie where the ground's baked so hard. I'd sooner take you in alive and hand you over to the hangman!"

"Go to hell, Long!" Batson shouted back. "I'd as lief be dead now as back in that stinking pen, waiting to swing!"

Batson underlined his choice to fight it out by triggering off another shot. Longarm ducked, and his move saved him, but cost him his hat. The rifle slug caught the edge of the Stetson where the felt of its crown formed a double thickness. The hat flew off Longarm's head and landed in the dirt a dozen feet behind him.

In spite of the near-hit, Longarm still held his fire. The veteran of more such standoffs than he liked to remember, Longarm had nerves of steel. Long ago he'd learned the trait that was common to so many cornered killers, the impatience that urges them to bull ahead in spite of danger and finish a gunfight as quickly as possible. Longarm made no move to retrieve his hat. Sooner or later, he knew Batson was sure to make the unwary move that would provide him with an almost certain target, and he had no intention of missing the opportunity.

Longarm's judgment proved as sound in this gun-duel as it had in so many others. Batson began working his way along the wall that sheltered him, and Longarm had no trouble following the killer's movements by watching the cracks in the barn wall darken as Batson edged slowly past them. By the time the killer had covered a dozen feet, he'd discovered that many of the open spaces between the boards were wide enough to allow him to slip his rifle-barrel between them.

Longarm saw the muzzle of the weapon slide into view through one of the cracks and ducked his head just in time to allow Batson's shot to be wasted as the bullet whistled harmlessly through empty air. A few yards farther along the wall, the fugitive tried a second similar shot, but again the very narrowness of the gap forced him to move so slowly that Longarm had plenty of time to drop below the edge of the protecting timber before his antagonist could squeeze off a shot.

Following the murderer's shadow, Longarm drew a bead on the next wide crack Batson would pass, but saw at once that the slit between the two thick boards was not wide enough to keep a rifle slug from being deflected by the boards' edges. Having no shells to waste, Longarm decided to hold his fire until he was certain of having a slug go home. The last thing he wanted was a wounded prisoner to nurse to the nearest railroad.

Digging into his vest pocket, Longarm fished out one of his cheroots and lighted it. From the way his chase had ended, he was sure that his wait would be prolonged. Batson was too old a hand at gunfighting to make a foolish move this early in the game.

By the time Longarm had taken two or three puffs of the cheroot, Batson had reached the end of the barn wall and started retracing his steps. Longarm watched, knowing that time was on his side. He was positive his patience would be greater than that of his quarry.

Suddenly the outline of the fugitive's body vanished from the cracks between the boards. Longarm frowned, trying to figure out what sort of move Batson might be making. Even as his brow puckered thoughtfully his question was answered. There was a sudden thudding of hoofbeats on packed earth, and the fugitive killer's horse galloped out of the shelter of the decrepit barn.

Batson was crouching forward in the saddle, his feet drumming his mount's flanks as he reined toward the skeleton of the house where Longarm was sheltered. The outlaw held his rifle in his right hand, his pistol in his left. The rifle cracked and its slug thudded into the timbers that shielded Longarm. Then the onrushing convict reared erect in his saddle and brought up his revolver, but before he could level it for a close-range shot that would have brought Longarm down, his instant of surprise had passed.

At last the convict had given Longarm the opportunity he'd been sure would present itself. With Batson only a few yards distant, Longarm did not have time to draw his Colt or to shoulder his Winchester and aim. He simply raised the rifle's muzzle and fired the weapon like it was a pistol. The recoil of his first shot sent the rifle's barrel up, but even before he could level the rifle for a second shot Longarm knew that it would not be necessary.

Batson's finger closed around the trigger of his revolver in his dying reflex. By some quirk of fate the bullet hit the hat where it rested on the ground. Then the impact of the Winchester's slug fired at such close range knocked the attacking outlaw from his saddle. Batson was dead before his body tumbled to the ground.

Looks like you made a real bad guess this time, old son, Longarm told himself silently. *Either that Batson misjudged how easy a target he was going to be, or he was ready to let himself get killed before he'd go back to jail and wait to take his last walk up to the hangman. Whichever was it was, he ain't going to do no more killing, that's for sure.*

On his way back to his horse, Longarm stopped to pick up the hat that the dead man's rifle slug had knocked off his head. He slid his finger through the holes made by the rifle bullet.

Well, it was getting to be time when you'd have to buy a new hat anyways, he mused, gazing at the fingertip that protruded through the hole in the Stetson's crown, then at the nick in the brim that the revolver bullet had cut. *But a miss is still a miss. It don't make no never-mind whether it's from a rifle or a handgun, or whether it goes wide by a country mile or just half of an inch.*

Donning the hat, Longarm slid his Winchester into its saddle-scabbard, walked on to the riderless horse standing beside Batson's body, and heaved the dead killer across its saddle. Then he led the horse to where his own mount waited, swung up onto its back, and started the long ride back to the railroad.

Now, standing in his room in the soft early morning light, Longarm fingered the bullet hole in the Stetson again. He shook his head thoughtfully, tossed the hat back on the dresser, and had another sip of Tom Moore before starting to dress for the day. A quarter of an hour later, he left the rooming house and started toward the Cherry Creek bridge.

During the short time it had taken him to dress, the light sprinkle of rain had passed over. Longarm crossed the bridge and turned east on Colfax Avenue. The sun was just beginning to bring out the gold dome on the Colorado state capitol building as he walked steadily toward Denver's downtown section. When he passed the closed door and shuttered window of George Masters's barbershop, his hand went up instinctively to rub the stubble that was beginning to show on his square jaws, but he reminded himself that this wouldn't be the first time Billy Vail and the others at the office had seen him when he needed a shave.

Besides, he was going to have to leave the office sometime during the morning to buy a new hat, and there'd be plenty of time then to have a late breakfast after he'd stopped for a shave at one of the downtown barbershops. His train hadn't gotten in until after midnight, and the free lunch he'd eaten at the saloon where he stopped on the way home had diminished his usual hunger for breakfast.

Strolling along unhurriedly, Longarm savored the fresh morning air, watching as Denver came to life after a night of rest. He reached the Federal Building and stretched his long muscular legs a bit longer than usual to mount the marble steps to the doorway two at a time. Taking a side stairway to the second floor, he opened the office door and entered his own familiar surroundings.

At the desk beside the door, Henry, the pink-cheeked clerk, looked up from the trial transcript he was reading.

"Well, I know the chief marshal will be glad to see you back, Marshal Long," he said. "He was remarking just yesterday that you must've taken a very slow train from wherever you were up in Dakota Territory."

"There ain't all that many trains to catch up there," Longarm replied. "And the depots ain't real close together, either. I guess Billy's in his office already?"

"He just got back from the telegraph room in the basement," the clerk answered. "But he didn't say anything about not wanting to be disturbed, so I guess it'll be all right for you to go on in, unless you want to read this letter first."

"Now, who'd I get a letter from?"

"I didn't open it, so I can't say," Henry replied, opening a drawer of his desk and taking out an amber-colored envelope. "It came a few days after you'd left on your case. But whoever it was must be pretty well-fixed, because the envelope shows they wrote it while they were staying at the Palace Hotel in San Francisco."

Taking the letter, Longarm stepped over to the window and opened it. Even though it was written on hotel stationery, he

7

recognized the faint familiar scent of Julia Burnside's perfume. He unfolded the single page and read.

"Longarm, my dear," the letter began, "I'm hoping that your cases will keep you close to your office for a month or so. I'll be leaving San Francisco in about two weeks, and plan to stop at our house in Denver for several days. As soon as I know exactly when I'll arrive, I'll send you a wire. Love, Julia."

Though he felt very much like smiling, Longarm kept a straight face while he folded the note and replaced it in its envelope. Then he crossed the outer office with long strides, tapped perfunctorily on Vail's office door, and opened it without waiting for his chief to reply.

Vail looked up from the sheaf of flimsies he was leafing through and said, "I was beginning to wonder when you'd show up. It's been almost a week since I got your telegram saying you'd closed your case. Did you take your prisoner to the pen at Leavenworth instead of bringing him back here with you?"

"Now, you got to be joshing me, Billy," Longarm told Vail. "Trains is scarce as hen's teeth up where I been at. And I didn't bring Charlie Batson back with me. He decided he'd rather shoot it out with me than give up when I told him to, so I had to kill him."

Vail's expression did not change. He nodded and said, "I had a hunch that'd be the outcome when you caught up with him. He always was too quick on the draw." His eye caught the hole in Longarm's hat and he went on, "And he also had a bad habit of shooting just a mite high. I suppose it was Batson who put that hole in your Stetson?"

"Oh, it was him, all right. I'd got him into a corner he couldn't get out of, and he figured he'd rather swap shots with me than surrender peaceful."

"At least that'll save the government a hangman's fee," Vail said. "And whatever it'd cost to keep him until he took his last walk to the gallows."

"Well, I was about due a new hat," Longarm said, taking off the Stetson and looking at the bullet hole. "I guess it'll be all right for me to put through a voucher for a new one."

"You know the rules as well as I do," Vail replied. "And I've still got to go by the book. Any personal wearing apparel damaged or destroyed in line of duty can be put on your expense voucher."

"You don't figure I'd put a hole in my own hat just to get Uncle Sam to buy me a new one, do you, Billy?"

"I've stopped trying to guess what you'd do, Long," Vail smiled. "Go on and get your new hat. And when I sign your expense voucher, I won't say a word to you about keeping your head down when you're standing in front of an outlaw with a gun. I suppose that's the way it was when you caught up with him?"

"Pretty much," Longarm nodded. "But it'll all be in my report when I write up the case." He pulled a chair up to the corner of Vail's desk and sat down. "Anyways, I was figuring on buying a new one, even if a new Stetson does cost six dollars now instead of four."

"Everything gets more expensive all the time," Vail agreed. "But do me a favor and get a new hat just like the one you've got on now. You've been wearing that one for something like ten years that I know of, and I'm not sure I'd recognize you if you got one that was a different shape or color."

"Now, you're joshing me, Billy," Longarm said. "But you don't need to worry. I ain't about to change the kinda crease I've got used to. Fact of the matter is, the only reason I was going to buy a new hat is so I wouldn't look like a saddle tramp when I go on my month of courtroom duty next week."

"That's something I haven't had time to mention yet," Vail said. "You won't be going on courtroom duty next week."

"Now, wait a minute, Billy!" Longarm protested. "You showed me the duty roster before I took off after Batson. And you said I was way overdue a spell of not doing anything but setting in court because I been on so many cases that's kept me travelling so much."

"That's still true," Vail nodded. "You're way overdue for a stretch of courtroom work. But you're going to have to wait another month, when I make up the new duty roster."

"I don't guess you'd mind telling me why you changed your mind?" Longarm asked. Because I got a—" He stopped short before mentioning the note he'd just gotten from Julia Burnside, and waited for the chief marshal to answer.

"Not a bit," Vail said. "This morning's session down in the telegraph room didn't amount to much, but there was one wire from Washington that I've got to act on right now."

"I take it that means I'm going out again?"

"I'm afraid it does," Vail told him. He began leafing through the sheaf of telegraph flimsies. "But this is a case I don't think you're going to mind taking on. One of the deputies from the Fort Smith office is missing. Judge Parker's worried about him, and he's asked Washington to have you assigned to the job of finding him."

Chapter 2

"Why'd Judge Parker pick on me?" Longarm asked.

"You remember a case you handled over in the Indian Nation a while ago? When you spooked out that bunch of bounty hunters?"

"Oh, sure," Longarm nodded. "That was when I met Judge Parker myself."

"Wasn't Jim Houlihan with the judge's special force of marshals then?"

"Seems to me he was," Longarm agreed. "I recall one young fellow called Jim. Had a big scar on his cheek, if I remember rightly, got it from some drunk half-breed Kiowa that went after him with a knife when Houlihan started to arrest him. He was still wet behind the ears, but he had the makings of a pretty good man. That was a while back, so I imagine he's growed up some by now."

"From the fuss Judge Parker's making about him, I'd say he sets a lot of store in Jim Houlihan."

"Oh, this fellow I was talking about had plenty of spunk, even if he was green. But as I recall, it wasn't such a much of a job to nosey out them bounty hunters and get 'em corraled."

"Maybe not. Judge Parker must remember how you took charge of things, how you cleared up the mess his own deputies had made. The judge has asked very specifically for you to be put on this case."

"And that sorta leaves you caught between a rock and a hard place, don't it, Billy?" Longarm asked.

"I've been between them before," Vail shrugged. "I'm not used to laying awake nights worrying about it."

"From what I heard, old Judge Parker stands pretty high in the Justice Department right now," Longarm went on. "I guess he can get just about anything he wants from them friends of his in Washington."

"That's one way you could put it," Vail replied slowly. "I don't know what kind of strings the old fellow pulls back there, but he's sure got a habit of getting his way when he sets his foot down."

"Well, I never bucked outa taking on a case yet," Longarm told Vail. "And I sure don't aim to start now. When did you say I'd have to go to Fort Smith?"

"I don't recall saying anything about a time schedule," Vail replied. "As a matter of fact, you might not have to go there at all."

"Somebody's got to tell me what the case is all about, Billy. You done enough work before you got shut up in this office to know that."

"What I'm saying is that Jim Houlihan didn't disappear from Fort Smith," Vail went on. "He was on a case in the field when he just dropped out of sight."

"Now, Billy, you know I got to dig into this job by going back to where it started," Longarm objected.

"I'm sure you'll do what you have to," Vail said. "And I've put in enough time in the field to know that nine times out of ten you've got to go over a lot of background, dig into the case until you find out how everything fits together. But this one's a little bit different."

"I don't see how, Billy, if you'll excuse me saying so,"

Longarm replied. His voice was thoughtful. "If Judge Parker sent Jim Houlihan or any other deputy marshal out on a case, whoever he sent would have to know all about it."

"Judge Parker would've given Houlihan all the background of any case that he put him on," Vail said patiently. "But your case is to find Jim Houlihan, and it starts at the place where he just dropped out of sight."

"And where was that?"

"Why—" Vail stopped short, frowning. "It was mentioned in the message that came from Washington today, I'm sure. I was reading over the telegrapher's shoulder while he was writing down what his key was bringing in, but for the life of me I don't recall the name of the place where Houlihan was when he sent in his last report. Wait just a minute while I look."

Picking up the stack of flimsies from his desk, the chief marshal started leafing through them. His frown deepened as he turned the pages until at last he found what he'd been searching for and lifted his head to look at Longarm.

"I was sure I'd seen it in here," Vail said. "And I was right. The place where Houlihan sent his report from is called Tonkawa, it's up in the north part of the Indian Nation."

"Sure, I know where that is," Longarm nodded. "It's right up close to the Kansas line, at the forks of the Arkansas River. That's Cherokee territory up there."

While Longarm was talking Vail had continued to leaf through the telegraph flimsies. He looked up now and said, "Then there was one more report. Houlihan mailed it at Tascosa."

"And that was the last one he sent in?"

"More than a month ago. But in that report, Houlihan mentioned having a clue he intended to follow and said he figured to make a big jump west because he had a pretty good idea where his man was heading."

"Which could've been anywhere he'd have some safe place he'd know about to hole up in."

"Of course. But before you tell me how much territory that could cover, there's one thing more I got in my messages from Washington this morning. Judge Parker asked the Justice Department auditor to go back over the travel vouchers they'd

13

gotten back from the railroads with Houlihan's signature on them."

"I've used that stunt myself," Longarm nodded. "Trouble is, they're always a month or two behind time."

"Just the same, they help," Vail said. "Now, Houlihan's last voucher was only six weeks old. He'd used it on the Denver & Rio Grande, for a trip from Trinidad to Alamosa."

"So that's how Judge Parker's case got into our jurisdiction," Longarm nodded. "I was wondering when you'd get around to telling me."

"Damn it, Long, this case is a mixed-up mess!" Vail exclaimed. "All I can do is tell you a little bit here and there. It's going to be up to you to fit all the pieces together and find out where Jim Houlihan is or what's happened to him."

"Oh sure. I've understood that from the beginning, Billy. Except I'm trying to figure out why Houlihan jumped around so much, like a flea on a hot griddle."

"I've seen you do the same thing," Vail pointed out.

"I reckon I know that even better'n you do," Longarm replied. "And I guess you done it, too, when you was working out in the field. But all this confabulating ain't got us to the point yet. What kind of case was Houlihan working on?"

"Didn't I mention that?" Vail frowned. "Houlihan was after Gunge Peyton."

"He's the one they call Bloodhand?"

"That's the only Gunge Peyton who was ever on our Wanted list, as far as I remember."

"You mean Gunge ain't been hung yet? Why, if I recall rightly, he was supposed to walk up the gallows steps more'n two months ago," Longarm said.

"He was, but he got away when the guards were moving him across the prison yard from the main cellblock to the one where they keep the prisoners waiting to be executed."

Longarm frowned. "I don't recall hearing about that."

"You were out in the field then, on that case down in Texas," Vail said. "And I guess nobody—including me—thought about mentioning it to you, because you had to leave right away on that new case up in Wyoming Territory."

"Well, if Houlihan went out after Gunge Peyton, he ought

14

not've had much trouble following him, unless Bloodhand changed his ways a lot since I tangled with him. That bragging trick he had of dipping his finger in the blood of anybody he killed and making an X with it on their foreheads was a dead giveaway to anybody trying to run him down," Longarm said thoughtfully.

"Unless he realized that those X's left a trail anybody could follow with no trouble at all," Vail suggested. "And from what I recall of him, Peyton's smart enough to figure that out."

"So is Judge Parker," Longarm put in.

"He sure doesn't miss much," Vail agreed. "I noticed in those reports he'd sent to Washington that he mentioned Gunge's bad habit of marking the men he'd shot. He asked them to report to him any cases they'd run into of killings where the body bore Peyton's mark."

"But they wouldn't get reports back in Washington of every killing in the country, Billy!" Longarm protested.

"Oh, I realize the reports aren't likely to help much," Vail agreed. "I'm sure the judge does, too. That's why you're going out."

"I guess I'll have time to buy me a new Stetson before I leave," Longarm said. "If you don't mind, I'll go take care of that, and then come on back here."

"It'll save time if you do that," Vail nodded. "I've got to go through this file of telegraph material before I can help you much in this case."

"It ain't going to take me long to pick out a hat, Billy, because I want one just like the one that got shot up. I'll be back inside of a half-hour or so."

Longarm was in no hurry. He strolled over to Seventeenth Avenue and turned in at the Daniels & Fisher department store. The store was almost without customers at this early hour, the clerks busy tidying up their merchandise. A sign suspended from the ceiling identified the men's department, and only a step from the main aisle he saw a section where hats were displayed.

Round-topped derbies, black, brown, and gray, sat atop tall stands, but there were no wide-brimmed Stetsons in sight.

Longarm stood for a moment gazing at the hats and was turning away when a young clerk bustled up.

"Can I be of service, sir?" he asked.

"You can, if you got some hats besides them over there,"
Longarm replied, indicating the derbies.

"But, sir, those derbies are the very latest style!" the clerk
exclaimed. "We imported them from London, England, especially for our customers. I'm sure you won't find a selection
like that in any other store in Denver!"

"That's as may be," Longarm replied, "but I ain't about to
put on one of 'em. Now, if you got a good Stetson just like the
one I got on, maybe we can do business."

"We have other hats, of course," the clerk replied as he
examined Longarm's battered headgear. "If you'll just step
over this way, I'm sure we can find something that will suit
you."

Longarm followed the clerk to a counter, where he stood
waiting while the young man took box after box of Stetsons
from below the counter and began opening them. In a very
short time the top of the counter was covered with hats in all
shades from pearly-white to midnight black, but there was not
a tobacco-brown hat among them.

"I'm sure we must have a Stetson that will suit you, sir,"
the clerk frowned after he'd emptied the last box. "Perhaps
you won't mind waiting just a moment, while I go look in the
stockroom?"

"Well, I ain't in no special hurry, but I ain't got all day,
either," Longarm frowned.

"I'll only be a moment," the young man promised.

"Go ahead, then. I'll wait."

Lighting a cigar while he leaned against the counter and
waited for the clerk to return, Longarm's mind turned to the
new case on which Billy Vail had just put him.

*This ain't going to be no easy one, old son. There's too
damn many maybes and ifs about where Houlihan might've
gone and when and why he shifted around so much. But being
as how the last place anybody knows he went to was Alamosa,
that's got to be where you better start from.*

Longarm's train of thought was interrupted by the clerk's

return. The young man was carrying a tobacco-brown Stetson. It had no crease in it, the brim was curved at its outer edge, and the crown looked twice as high as the one Longarm had on.

"I'm afraid this is the only brown Stetson we have in stock," he said apologetically. "Of course, we can always order one from the factory, but it takes from three weeks to a month for us to get special orders like that."

"Well, suppose I try it on and see how it fits," Longarm suggested. He took off his battered and bullet-pierced hat and laid it on the counter, then donned the stiff new one the clerk handed him. It was a bit too large, and the high pointed crown towered above him like a miniature mountain when he looked at himself in the full-length mirror that rose beside the counter. Turning back to the clerk, he said, "It's a mite too big, but I guess I can fold up some paper and put it in the sweatband. And I sure don't like the way that brim curves up. It'll let the sun shine right into my eyes when I'm heading into it."

"Why, we can take care of that for you," the clerk told him. "We have a steam press in the basement. It'll shrink the hat to your exact size, flatten the brim, and put a crease in the crown that will be an exact copy of the one you're wearing now."

"You sure about that?"

"Oh, absolutely! We adjust hats for our customers every week. But it'll take a little time, and if you don't care to wait, I'll have to ask you to leave the hat you're wearing now so we can size the new one properly."

"That'd mean I got to walk back to my office bareheaded!" Longarm objected. "Why, everybody I passed on the street'd be looking at me like I'm crazy! You go ahead and do what you need to so's the new one'll fit. I'll wait. I got some thinking to do, anyways, so it won't put me out none."

An hour later, the new brown hat sitting jauntily on his head but feeling stiff and unfamiliar, Longarm walked into the office again. Henry looked up and whistled.

17

"That hat looks very nice indeed, Marshal Long," he said. "It certainly is better than your old one."

"Oh, I ain't thrown the old one away," Longarm said. "The fellow at the store said he could fix it up almost as good as new for me, so I'll have it for a spare."

"Well, the chief marshal said for you to go right on in when you got back. He said he has some new information about the case."

With a nod of thanks, Longarm crossed the outer office to Vail's door and entered without knocking.

"That new hat's a real improvement," he commented. "Your old one was beginning to look battered."

"Maybe it's a good thing you like it," Longarm replied. "I figured on paying seven dollars, but by the time they finished fooling around with it at the store so's it'd fit just right and then fixing up my old one so's I can wear it again, I'll have to put through a voucher for close to nine dollars."

"I promised you I wouldn't josh you about not keeping your head down, so I'm not going to say a word," Vail said. "Fill out your voucher and give it to the clerk. I'll sign it."

"Well, thanks, Billy," Longarm nodded. "For the hat, I mean."

"No thanks needed," Vail told him.

"I guess you had plenty of time by now to go through all that stuff you got over the telegraph wire this morning?"

"I've read it word for word. And I didn't find out anything beyond what I've already told you. There were some remarks Judge Parker put in that I hadn't remembered, but there wasn't anything in them that'd help you find out where his missing man might've gone."

"I had a sorta hunch that'd be the case," Longarm nodded. "I'll just have to pick up his trail at Alamosa and follow along until I catch up with him."

Vail nodded. "The clerk's got your travel orders and vouchers ready, and I've authorized an extra fifty dollars in travel money for this case, since Houlihan is one of the men from our own force."

"Now, that's real thoughtful of you, Billy," Longarm nodded. "Seeing as how it's still a week till payday and I'm a mite short of cash money. If I leave right now, I can get back to my rooming house and dig my dirty laundry outa my travel gear and pack up again and still make the afternoon train."

Longarm stopped only long enough to send a telegram to Julia Burnside, telling her that he'd had to leave on a special case and might be out of town when she passed through Denver. He invited her to let him know of her next trip. Then he walked with long strides to his rooming house.

Longarm wasted little time in packing. The afternoon train on the Denver & Rio Grande was due to pass through Denver at four o'clock, and though it would put him into Alamosa in the dead hours between midnight and dawn, he intended to be on it instead of waiting for the morning train the next day. He crammed a spare pair of longjohns and a freshly laundered shirt into his saddlebags, added a change of socks and an extra supply of ammunition for both his Winchester and Colt. Since he hadn't unpacked any of his other needs, he closed the flaps, cinched down the straps, and was ready to travel.

Carrying his saddlebags over one shoulder, his bedroll over the other, and his rifle in his left hand, Longarm reached the D&RG depot just in time to exchange his first travel voucher for a ticket to Alamosa before the train arrived. There were few passengers in the daycoaches, and Longarm found his favorite seat still vacant—the seat at the end of the last passenger coach, which was also the smoker.

Settling down onto the green plush upholstery, he took out a cheroot and lighted it. Through the veil of smoke he watched the houses of Denver thinning out as the train gained speed through the suburbs that were beginning to spring up around the outskirts of the growing city.

Well, old son, he told himself silently, *looks like you got a real job on your hands this time. There ain't no way of telling where Jim Houlihan's got off to by now. Best thing you can do is just pick up on whatever trail he's left and dog along on it till you catch up with him, regardless of how long it takes.*

Chapter 3

"I ain't sure how long I'll be staying here," Longarm told the sleepy-eyed stationmaster at the Alamosa depot. He had been one of two passengers who'd gotten off the train. The other had been a man who wasted no time in heading for the buildings of the little town that stretched away from the tracks. Longarm was standing just inside the depot door, his saddlebags and bedroll at his feet. "You got a cubbyhole of some kind where I can put this gear for a little while, so it'll be safe?"

"Right where it's laying is as good a place as any," the trainsman replied.

"If I leave my rifle, you figure it'll be safe here, too?"

"Sure. Soon as the train finishes taking on water, I'll lock up and go back to bed. I won't open up the depot till about an hour before the day train's due, tomorrow just before noon."

"You sleep here every night, then?"

"Mister, as far as I'm concerned, this is home. That's my

bedroom, right over there." The stationmaster pointed across the waiting room to a door that stood ajar. "In a little place like this, only two trains a day, the D&RG ain't wasting money by hiring two damn fools like me."

"If that's the case, I'll just let my stuff stay right where it is," Longarm said. "But I guess I better tell you, I'll be back to get it soon as the livery stable opens up, so likely I'll be rousing you up before too long."

"Come back whenever you want to. I wake up easy and I go back to sleep just the same way."

Longarm went out of the depot and walked across a short stretch of hard gravelly dirt to Alamosa's main street. Though midnight had long since passed and daybreak lay only a few hours ahead, yellow rectangles of lamplight still showed above and below the swinging doors of a three or four saloons. He picked the one with the brightest light and angled across the street toward its doors.

Pushing through the batwings, he flicked his eyes over the almost-deserted room as he started for the bar. There were two men at the far end of the mahogany, arguing halfheartedly while the barkeep looked on. Men were sprawled in chairs at two of the half-dozen tables that stood along the opposite wall, their heads resting on the tables, obviously sleeping off their liquor. When he saw Longarm push through the swinging doors, the barkeep started along the bar toward him.

"What's your pleasure, mister?" the saloon-keeper asked around the half-smoked stub of a cigar clamped between his teeth.

"I'd take right kindly to a tot of Maryland rye," Longarm replied. He laid a cartwheel on the mahogany. "Tom Moore, if you happen to have a bottle."

"Can't accommodate you with Moore, but I got some Drummonds that's just about as good."

"I'll make do with it," Longarm nodded. "And pour yourself one, too, while you're at it."

"No thanks, friend. I've had just about all I can handle tonight. But I'll take a cigar, if it's all the same to you."

"Help yourself," Longarm nodded.

Though he knew that as soon as he was gone the barkeep

would put the cigar back in the box and take its price from the till, he considered the dime he was paying a small sum if it brought him the information he hoped to get.

Just as Longarm had thought would be the case, the barkeep set a shot-glass and bottle in front of him, then made a show of picking out a cigar from one of the boxes on the backbar and sliding it into his vest pocket.

"Just got off the night train, I guess?" he asked as he turned back to Longarm.

"Yep," Longarm answered as he filled his glass. Among the many lessons he'd learned during his long years as a lawman was to avoid asking too many questions too quickly in a strange town unless an emergency demanded immediate action. Speaking in an off-hand manner, he went on, "I ain't been in Alamosa for a long time. From the little bit I could see in the dark, it ain't changed much."

"I don't guess it will for a while, either. Just about all the good farmland hereabouts has been claimed by now."

"It's a pretty quiet little town, ain't it?" Longarm asked casually after he'd drained his glass. He reached for the bottle to refill the glass as he went on, "Don't get many strangers passing through town?"

"Not many. You looking for somebody in particular?"

"Matter of fact, I am. I was wondering—"

"Lawman, ain't you?" the barkeep broke in. "Or maybe a bounty-hunter?"

Now that the barkeep had made a successful guess, Longarm saw no reason to dodge the question. He said, "Deputy U. S. marshal, outa the Denver office. I'm trying to track down another fellow off our force. He seems to've got as far as Alamosa, then just dropped outa sight."

"How long's he been missing?"

"Oh, maybe a month, give or take a few days. He's a young fellow, got a big scar from a knife-cut on his cheek. His name's Jim Houlihan."

Pursing his lips, the barkeep shook his head. "I don't recall seeing him. I know most of the locals, so I'd likely remember it if I had, with his face marked up like you say. Maybe one of the day men noticed him, but he'd've been as likely to go into one of the other saloons as to come in here."

"Oh, I'm just starting out," Longarm said. "I'll pretty well cover the town before I get through."

"You government men sure stick together, don't you?"

"I guess we do," Longarm agreed. "Maybe that's on account of there ain't too many of us, and there's a lot of outlaws that's got a habit of running in gangs these days."

"Well, I wish I could help you, Marshal, but I sure don't recall anybody with a scarred face that I ain't seen before." The barkeep picked up Longarm's cartwheel, bent down for a moment and fumbled under the bar, then put a half-dollar in front of Longarm. He asked, "Have you asked Buck Saunders about him? Buck runs the livery down at the end of the street."

"Not yet, but I'll get there before I'm through. And now, if you'll answer me one more question, I'll be moving along."

"Ask away."

"I guess you got some kind of town officer? Marshal or policeman or constable?"

"Jack Grassley. He's the constable. If you're going down the street, you'll likely run into him. He ain't been in here yet tonight, but when he comes in I'll tell him you'd like to talk to him."

"Thanks kindly," Longarm nodded, picking up his change. "I'll be around town for a few hours yet."

Before the night had died completely, Longarm had visited the other three saloons without finding any Tom Moore rye whiskey or uncovering any evidence that Jim Houlihan had passed through Alamosa.

Daybreak was tinting the eastern sky, a brightening gray outlining the sloping peaks that marked the end of the Rocky Mountains' eastern spur, when he turned back from the end of the street and started toward the depot. The livery stable had been closed, its windows dark, and Longarm's stomach was reminding him that he'd had nothing to eat since an early supper when the train had stopped at Trinidad. He reached the saloon where he'd started his investigation just as a chubby middle-aged man pushed through the batwings and stepped off the board sidewalk to the street.

He looked at Longarm for a moment, then called, "Just a minute! Are you the federal marshal that's looking for me?"

"Well, I wasn't exactly tearing up your town trying to find you," Longarm replied, changing his course down the street and angling across it to where the chubby man had stopped. "But I'd guess you're Jack Grassley, and I do want to swap a word or two with you, if you got time."

"Nothing but time," the other man replied. "I'm Grassley, and I'm just winding up my night's work. If you ain't had breakfast yet, I'm going over to Ma Simpson's boarding-house. It's just a step or two off Main Street here, and we can talk while we're eating."

As he reached the constable, Longarm extended his hand and said, "My name's Long, I work outa the Denver office, and—"

"Wait a minute!" Grassley broke in. "You'd be the federal marshal they call Longarm, am I right?"

"Some folks call me that," Longarm admitted.

"Well, now! I'm right glad to meet you," Grassley went on. "I've sure heard a lot about you."

"One thing I can't do is stop people from talking," Longarm said as walked beside Grassley, letting the other man lead the way by a half-step. "And I don't aim to take up your time with a lot of useless palaver. The case I'm on here is to find a deputy out of the Arkansas jurisdiction that's turned up missing."

"I'm afraid I can't help you much on that," Grassley said, frowning. "You're the first outside lawman I know of that's come here in the last six or seven months."

"I'm real sure Houlihan was here, too, but I ain't sure when," Longarm said as he followed Grassley into a white-painted frame house. He let the constable lead the way through a kitchen in which the smell of frying bacon hung heavily, and into a room dominated by a big dining table set squarely in its center. An aproned woman, well past middle age, was putting plates and utensils on the table.

"I brought another lawman to have breakfast with me, Miz

Simpson," Grassley said. "His name's Long. He's a federal marshal outa Denver. I guess you got enough food for both of us without shorting anybody else."

"Now, did you ever see me run out of food, Jack Grassley?" she replied. "I'm right pleased Jack brought you with him, Marshal Long. You men set down and I'll serve you right off. I'll bet both of you are starving."

"I'll admit I'm more'n a mite hungry," Longarm told her as he followed Grassley to the table. "And I'll bet you're a good cook, too."

"If you say that after you've had breakfast, then I'll believe you," she smiled. "Now you men set down and I'll get your breakfast and then I'll get out of your way so's you can talk."

Longarm and Grassley did very little talking until they'd taken the edge off their appetites with fried eggs and bacon and biscuits hot from the oven. When their hunger had been satisfied, Grassley turned to Longarm.

"You said you're looking for this federal marshal out of Arkansas, Marshal Long. I wish I could help you, but like I told you, if this man you're after came through here, I sure didn't see him or hear anything about him."

"Oh, he was here, all right, even if all I got to go on is an expense voucher he give the railroad line for a ticket here from Trinidad," Longarm frowned. "There ain't no way to find out when he used it, but he must've come here or there wouldn't be no voucher."

"And the man he was after?" Grassley asked.

"There's not any way to find out about him. He's a killer that cheated the hangman by making a getaway from the pen. I'm just gambling that Houlihan got a line on him, and was following whatever clues he had to keep on his trail."

"You know the D&RG turns south and heads down into New Mexico from here, so he could've just stopped between trains," Grassley suggested. "And some hires horses if they're only going a little ways, like to the Ute reservation on further west. Maybe that's what this Houlihan did."

"He could've gone either way, I guess," Longarm agreed. "All I know is that he ain't been heard from after he left here.

26

But I'm not counting too much on the man Houlihan was after going where there's a lot of people."

"Could he've been going to Green's Hole? That's to the northwest," Grassley told him.

"Maybe. I know where it is. I had a case there a few years back. But was it me going to Green's hideout, I'd've cut north before now," Longarm said with a thoughtful frown.

"This fellow your deputy marshal was after, was he maybe a half-breed that'd go to his own kind and get them to hide him?"

"Now, that's something I don't know," Longarm replied. "Why'd you ask?"

"Well, the Utes ain't peaceful yet," Grassley said. "If he had some Ute or Paiute blood, he'd likely look to his own kind to hide him."

"That's an idea that hadn't struck me," Longarm nodded. "How far's the Ute reservation from here?"

"Not far at all. It's only twenty miles or less to the Indian Agency headquarters."

"Which way does it lay?"

"The reservation's right at what folks hereabouts call the Four Corners, because it's the only place in the country where four boundary lines come together."

"I been there a time or two," Longarm nodded. "Colorado, New Mexico, Arizona, and Utah all join, and outlaws like it there because it's easy for 'em to get away from anybody but a federal lawman like me."

"That's right," Grassley agreed. "And the Ute lands spill over all four boundaries. My bet is that's where your man Houlihan's tracked whoever it is he's after."

"It wouldn't surprise me," Longarm said thoughtfully. "I guess I better get over there and start noseying around. You said it's on the Ute reservation, so I guess there's an Indian Agency office somewheres close by?"

"Just slant southeast when you ride outa here," Grassley replied. "There's a pretty good trail leading to it. You'll cross three creeks and two rivers, and the Indian Agency office is right alongside the trail."

"How much of a ride is it?" Longarm asked.

"It'll take you the better part of two days, even if you get started right away," Grassley said. "I guess you've got a horse?"

"No, but I've already found the livery stable down at the edge of town. I was aiming to ask if Jim Houlihan might've hired a horse when he left Alamosa, but I stopped by it before daylight and nobody was there."

"Well, Buck Saunders will be on the job by now, and he'll treat you right. He's got good animals, too."

Longarm stood up. "If I got a two-day ride ahead of me, I better get moving. I'll pay the landlady for our breakfast, and thanks for all your help."

"Why, Miz Simpson won't let you pay for breakfast," Grassley said. "Her husband was a lawman up in Dakota Territory, and she won't take a dime from anybody that wears a badge. Says she don't need no money and she owes lawmen too much to take theirs away from 'em."

"I never run into anybody before who felt like that," Longarm said. "But at least I got to thank her."

"You do that, when you pass through the kitchen," Grassley said. "And good luck to you. If you need some help down the road, send for me. I ain't as young and spry as I was when I was town marshal up in Deadwood."

"You never mentioned you was a lawman up there," Longarm said, not even trying to hide the surprised look on his face. "Was that before or after Wild Bill Hickock got killed?"

"Before. I give up the job to Bill. Me and him was pretty good friends, and I was getting a mite tired and slowing down."

"If you wore a badge in Deadwood, you are all right," Longarm told Grassley. "Maybe if I come back this way we can visit again."

"Sure. Be glad to," Grassley nodded. "Now, if you're going to get anyplace today, you better be starting."

Longarm touched the brim of his hat to Grassley and went into the kitchen. Mrs. Simpson was sitting at the table, stirring a bowl of pancake batter.

"I'd like to pay you for my breakfast," he told her.

"You mean that Jack Grassley didn't tell you I won't take any pay from lawmen?" she asked.

"He did, but I figured—"

"Well, you figured wrong," she broke in. "And I guess if Jack told you, he told you why I don't, too. Now, I know you must be here on some kind of case, so you just get along, but first pick up that lunch I packed for you. I heard you and Jack talking about you riding out right away, so don't try to put me off and say you won't be needing it."

"Why—" Longarm began, then stopped short. "Why, I do thank you again, Miz Simpson. And if I get back this way, I'll stop in and see you."

"You do that. And now, if you've got business to tend to, you'd better scoot on and do it."

After he'd left the house, Longarm lighted a cigar. The fresh breeze of early morning coiled its blue-gray smoke into spirals as he made his way to the depot. Loaded with his gear, he made his way down the awakening street to the livery stable. As Grassley had assured him it would be, the doors of its cavernous barn were open and a man was emptying feed from a grain sack into the long feeding trough that stretched along one side of the pole corral. Bending over the trough, he did not see Longarm.

"Morning!" Longarm called. "When you finish working there, I got to see about hiring a horse from you."

"That's what I'm in business for," the liveryman replied. "Come on in the corral, if you want to pick one out."

Leaving his gear where he was standing, Longarm ducked between the poles and joined the liveryman.

"My name's Long," he said. "Deputy U. S. marshal outa the Denver office."

"I'm Buck Saunders," the liveryman replied. "Now, you look over the nags in the corral here, and pick out whichever one you think you'd fancy."

"Before we start dickering up a deal, I got to ask you a question and tell you something," Longarm said. "First off, I need to know if you've rented a horse in the last month or so to another deputy marshal that answers to the name of Jim

Houlihan. He'd've paid you with an expense voucher, just like I'll have to do, but it's as good as cash, so—"

"Excuse me for butting in, Marshal Long," Saunders said. "I know how your vouchers work. I'll answer your question, too. I did rent a horse to another man from your department about a month ago, and his name was Jim Houlihan. Why? Are you trying to catch up to him? If you are, you'll have to move right fast, because he's got a mighty good start on you."

Longarm was staring at Saunders, surprised by the speed and completeness of the liveryman's reply. It wasn't often that he had such good luck, and he wasn't quite ready to believe that he'd hit on the trail of the missing deputy so easily.

"I better make sure we're talking about the same man," he said. "This Jim Houlihan, was there anything special you noticed about him?"

"Well, he was a young fellow," Saunders replied. "He had a big scar on one side of his face, and he showed me his badge. He said it might be a while before I'd get my horse back, because he was trailing a fugitive and didn't know how long it'd be before he caught up with him."

"That'd be Houlihan, all right," Longarm nodded. "I don't guess he said where he was going?"

Saunders shook his head. "Just that he was after a man who'd escaped from jail and was likely to be headed west. He described the man to me, but I hadn't seen him. He asked about the country ahead, and I told him as best I could. When he left, he rode off to the west. That's about all I can tell you."

"What you told me's a real help," Longarm said. "And you said Houlihan was here about a month ago?"

"Give or take a few days," Saunders nodded. "I can look on my ledger and tell you the day, if you're interested."

"I sure am!" Longarm exclaimed.

"We can go inside and look now, or you can pick out your horse first. I don't see any saddle gear with your stuff over there, but I can fix you up with a McClellan if you need one."

"That'll suit me to a tee," Longarm nodded. He looked at the half-dozen horses in the corral and pointed to a dun gelding. "That one over there looks like he'd be all right."

"He's a good trail horse. I'll just lead him up to the barn and get him saddled up."

"I'll be making out my voucher while you do that," Longarm said. "And I'll be on my way as fast as you get the horse saddled. Looks like I'm running about a month behind the man I'm after, and I don't want to waste a minute catching up!"

Chapter 4

In the far distance, Longarm caught a glimpse of sunlight reflected at ground level in a dazzling shine. He reined in and took his bandanna from his pocket to wipe away the drops of sweat that were dripping from his nose and chin. The sun was dropping into evening, but the air was hot, as it had been ever since he entered the desert-like *malpais* over which he'd been riding since the day before. The sky was cloudless, and the late afternoon sun was still bright. Its heat shimmered up from the baked ground and even though he'd kept the livery horse to a moderate walk, the small air current that his passing stirred had seemed even hotter than it was now that he'd stopped.

With sweat no longer dripping from his eyebrows and clouding his eyelashes, Longarm confirmed what he'd been sure was the source of the bright reflection. He could now make out the blocky outlines of several small adobe buildings that stood on the bottom of the saucer-like depression he had started to ride across almost an hour ago. The buildings were of the same light brownish hue as the ground they hugged, making them almost invisible even in the brilliant sunshine.

"But that's got to be the place," Longarm muttered. "And even if it ain't, there'll be folks there who can tell you where to find the place you're looking for."

Twitching the reins of the livery horse and touching the animal's flank with a boot heel, Longarm started toward the buildings.

Two full days had passed since Longarm had ridden out of Alamosa, and the third day was within a few hours of ending. The trail which had been well-beaten in the beginning had begun to grow dimmer by the middle of the second day, and disappeared almost completely when he encountered long expanses of reddish-purple lava rock. The patches had soon increased in area, and soon there was no longer earth under the horse's hooves, but an unstable covering of lava rock.

At times he'd had to dismount and lead the horse across stretches where the loose, porous chunks of crumbling lava caused the animal to stumble. In other spots, some a mile or more wide, the lava covered the ground in bits no bigger than a man's fingertip, and was almost as slippery and treacherous as small hailstones underfoot. Even if there had been heavy traffic across the lava bed, the crumbly volcanic stone would not have settled down and held traces of hoofprints or even wagon wheels.

Long before he had shortened the distance to the buildings, Longarm was able to make out details of the structures. One was substantially larger than the other three. Together with a small horse corral, they formed a group near the center of an area that was perhaps a mile in diameter, a place where through some freak of nature during the gigantic upheavals of volcanic activity in ages past an island of desert soil had remained untouched. A few weeds, invisible from a distance, had grown up around the edges of the buildings, and made a spot of green in an otherwise desolate area.

In spite of the shifting footing which slowed the progress of the livery horse, Longarm drew steadily closer to the buildings. When his horse at last stepped onto the hard-baked soil of the island of earth surrounded by lava, he began to feel better. He toed the animal into a faster walk and started studying the details of the houses.

One of the buildings was substantially larger than the others, and stood a bit apart from the cluster. Except for its size, it was no different from its neighbors, or from any of the other thick-walled, flat-roofed adobe brick dwellings common in the region. The most unusual feature the big building boasted was glass in its deep-set windows. He could now make out a sign above the door which opened in the center of the structure. The legend read: "U. S. Indian Bureau, Headquarters Ute/Paiute Reservation."

Well, old son, Longarm told himself, *looks like you hit square on target. Now let's see just how much good it's going to do you.*

The door of the headquarters building opened and a man came out. He wore the brown denim trousers and tan cotton shirt which Longarm had found to be the unofficial uniform of Indian Bureau field workers. The man was pushing middle age. He was not wearing a hat, and he was beginning to grow bald, a single strip of graying hair pushed down the center of his otherwise bare scalp. His nose was long and aquiline, his lips were thin, his cheeks high and his chin narrow.

Raising his voice, he called, "Ride on up and dismount. It's good to see a fresh face out here." As Longarm reined in and swung out of his saddle, the man stepped up and extended his hand. "I'm Cameron Collins," he went on. "The Indian agent. We don't get many visitors in this out-of-the-way place."

"Long's my name," Longarm said as they shook hands. "And we both got the same boss, Uncle Sam. I'm a Deputy U. S. marshal outa the Denver office."

"I hope you're not looking for one of my Indians," Collins frowned as he led the way to the headquarters building. "They've got their own police force, you know, and when a U. S. marshal shows up, I start to worry."

"Far as I know right now, you ain't got a thing to worry about," Longarm replied. "But until I do a little bit of digging, I can't be sure."

Collins led the way down a cool hallway, almost chilly now that they were out of the beating sun. He motioned Longarm into an opened door. The room they entered was as cool as the hall. Colorful Indian-woven blankets hung on three of the walls; the fourth was broken by the windows. Beneath them, crowded bookcases formed a solid tier to the wide floor planking. A paper-littered desk stood in front of the windows and a long sofa upholstered in leather stretched in front of the desk. Cameron motioned Longarm to the divan.

"Well, Marshal Long, suppose you tell me what's brought you here," the Indian agent suggested, settling into the chair behind the desk. "It must be something serious, since you've come all the way from Denver."

"Real serious," Longarm nodded. "There's a deputy marshal missing from Judge Parker's district over in Arkansas, and I'm trying to find out what happened to him."

"He wouldn't have any reason to come here, at least none that I can think of," Collins frowned. "The Utes have their own police force to keep order among their people, but I suppose you know that."

"Most reservations do," Longarm said. "But this deputy I'm looking for wasn't interested in your Utes. He was trailing a real bad one, a killer that escaped from the pen just before he was due to swing for murder. And I found out back in Alamosa that the deputy I'm looking for—Jim Houlihan's his name—started this way on the track of the man he was after."

"You said this Houlihan was missing," the agent frowned. "Do you mean he just dropped out of sight?"

"Sometime after he'd left Alamosa," Longarm told him. "His trail was clear to there. But he's been gone close to a month now, so Judge Parker got my chief to set me on his trail."

"Well, I certainly haven't seen him," Collins said. "As a matter of fact, you're the first stranger who's been here for almost three months. This place isn't easy to get to, but I'm sure you've found that out."

"It's a pretty far piece from anyplace," Longarm agreed. "And I ain't even sure Houlihan came onto your reservation.

All I know is that he left Alamosa heading west on whatever kinda trail the man he was after had left."

"My guess is that whoever your man was after headed up to Green's Hole. I'm sure you know about it."

Longarm nodded. "Sure. I been there a time or two myself. But I figure if he'd been going there, he'd've cut up to the north a long ways back. Besides, Jim Houlihan was heading this way, which he likely wouldn't've done unless he was on a pretty warm trail. I'm betting he started out for your place here."

"If he did, he never got here," Collins said. "Or if he got here, I didn't hear about him."

"From what I seen riding in, you ain't got much here that'd draw a man like that escaped killer Houlihan was after," Longarm frowned. "Where's all the Utes?"

"South and west of the lava beds," the agent replied. "In places where there's cropland. By rights, my headquarters should be closer to the Ute villages, but it was set up years ago when the Indian Bureau was first formed, and I've found out that nothing's as slow to move as a government bureau. I've been trying to get my superiors in Washington to let me move, but of course they've never been out here and don't have any idea how inconvenient it is."

"If you don't know anything that'll help me, I better keep moving and look someplace else for Jim Houlihan," Longarm said. "Trouble is, I don't know where to head out when I leave here. Looks like I've run into a dead end."

"Perhaps not," the man said. "Let me call Se-Na-Ha. She might've heard something from her people."

"This girl, she's a Ute, I guess?"

Cameron Collins nodded. "My eyes and ears in the tribe. She's very bright, speaks pretty good English, and I've learned to trust her. She lives in one of the hogans in back of the office." Rising, he started for the door. "It'll only take a minute for me to get her."

While he waited for the man to return, Longarm took out a fresh cigar and lighted it, then inspected his surroundings without seeing anything that particularly interested him. The

Indian agent was gone only a short time. When he came back, a young Indian girl was with him.

"This is the man I told you about, Se-Na-Ha," Collins said. "He works for the government, too, and he wants to ask you some questions."

Longarm looked at Se-Na-Ha for a moment before speaking to her. She was short and seemed round and stocky in the shapeless deerskin dress she wore. The garment was of the simplest cut and had a high neckline. It fitted closely across her shoulders, bulged out at her full breasts, then fell in an almost straight line from her shoulders to her calves. Had both of them been standing, Se-Na-Ha's head would have lacked an inch or two of reaching Longarm's shoulders.

Her face was broad, as was her rounded, stubby nose, and showed no lines of age. Though her cheekbones were high, the fullness of her cheeks and jaws and her flattened nose combined with wide pouting lips made her head look pumpkin-round. Her eyes, obsidian black, were framed in lids that had an almond shape, giving her face an almost Oriental cast. The sleeveless dress exposed her chubby arms almost to her shoulders, and Longarm looked at them twice before he was sure that they were not fat, but muscular. Like the skin of her face and neck, that on her arms was a deep brown.

"I'm looking for two men, not just one," Longarm told the Ute girl. "One of them's a killer who escaped from prison, the other one is a—" He hesitated for a moment, then went on, "He's an officer of the government, like Mr. Collins here, and like I am."

"I understand about officers," Se-Na-Ha nodded. The words in English came easily from her lips and her speech was almost totally without an accent. "I know about men who kill other men, too. You look for the one who has killed so you can take him to prison."

"That's right," Longarm agreed. "And I'm looking for the other one because he was trying to catch up with the killer and put him back in prison. He headed this way from Alamosa pretty near a month ago, and that's all we know."

"Why would I know more than you, then?" she asked.

"You know why quite well, Se-Na-Ha," Collins broke in.

38

"Your people seem to know about it any time a stranger sets foot on your reservation."

Se-Na-Ha shook her head. "If there is such a stranger, I have not been told."

"You always seem to know about such things as new people coming to the reservation," Collins insisted. "And if you don't know, I'm sure you can find out. They would be two men, the killer and another U. S. marshal."

"Is the man who kills one of our people?" the Ute girl asked, frowning.

"No, he's—" Longarm began, then stopped short and shook his head thoughtfully. "Well, he might have some Indian blood in him, at that. As I recall, he's from the Indian Nation, or real close to it."

"I will ask," Se-Na-Ha nodded. "And maybe tomorrow, maybe the next day, I will find out something."

"You do that," Longarm told her. He turned to Collins and went on, "I'd sorta like to scout around and see if I can come across some trace of Jim Houlihan or the man he was after, and it looks like that's going to take a little time. You reckon you could put me up someplace for a night or two?"

"Of course," the Indian agent replied. "There's plenty of room that I don't use unless one of the Agency's travelling inspectors is here, which isn't very often. And I'll be glad to have company. It's all too seldom that anybody outside the reservation stops and stays very long."

When Collins finished speaking, Se-Na-Ha asked, "You want to ask me more questions?"

"Not unless you got some answers," Longarm replied. "but if you'll try to find whether any of your people has seen anything of Jim Houlihan or that escaped killer he was following, I'd sure like to know about it."

"I will tell you, if I hear," Se-Na-Ha promised. Then, with a nod to Collins, she left the room.

Although the noise of his bedroom door opening and closing was only a faint whisper of sound, it was enough to rouse Longarm instantly. As he usually did in strange surroundings, he'd pulled a chair up beside the bed and hung his gunbelt over the back. Only the faintest light trickled in through the single small slit of a window set high in the bedroom wall.

Even as the door was opening, he snapped awake, fully alert, and reached for the well-worn grip of his Colt. The gun was in his hand, aimed and loaded, before he saw a shadowy form slipping into his room, outlined against the uncurtained window in the hall outside.

Longarm rolled catlike to the floor. Standing up in his longjohns he drew a bead at the blot of the dark form. As he leveled the revolver he said, "Stop right where you're at. I don't wanta pull the trigger of this sixgun I'm holding on you, but you better start talking quick, or I will."

A woman's voice came from the darkness, an urgent tone in its whispered words. "Do not shoot!" she said. "I have no gun. I came here only to talk."

"Se-Na-Ha?" Longarm asked, not sure that he recognized the voice of the Ute girl.

"Yes. I have things to say that I did not want to say where others might hear."

Not relaxing, but feeling relieved that the midnight intruder was not a murdering stranger, Longarm said, "Go on and talk, then. I'm listening."

By now Longarm's eyes had adjusted to the midnight blackness and he could make out Se-Na-Ha's form clearly outlined against the door's dark panels in the starlight's faint shine that came through the windows in the wide corridor. She was standing in the opening, motionless.

"It is very hard to begin," she said. "What I have to talk about is of importance to my family. It could be of great hurt to us if the agent should know."

"You're in some kinda trouble?" Longarm asked.

"I do not know," she replied. "This is what I want to ask you about."

"Well, if we're going to talk, I guess you better come on in the rest of the way and shut the door," he told her. "And I'll light the lamp so's we can see each other."

"No!" Se-Na-Ha said quickly. "There are never lights in the agent's house this late. If someone saw it they would be sure to think there was trouble here, to keep the agent up."

"All right," Longarm said. "We'll talk in the dark. But close the door first."

When Se-Na-Ha closed the door it shut out the light from the hall window, and the window in the room did not admit enough starshine to allow Longarm to see her except as a darker shadow in the gloom. Longarm rose from his crouched position and sat on the side of the bed. By habit he fished a cigar from the pocket of the vest that hung opposite his gun-belt on the chair-back and fumbled in the pocket for a match.

Longarm closed his eyes to keep from being blinded by the sudden light that flooded the pitch-dark room when the match flared into flame, then opened them a slit. Se-Na-Ha was still standing beside the door, and she closed her eyes when the match spurted flame.

"I guess you better set down," Longarm told her. He lighted his cheroot, then held the match high to let the Ute girl find a chair before blowing out the match and adding, "I got a feeling we're going to be talking for a spell."

"It will not take very long to tell you what I have come to say," Se-Na-Ha assured him. She sat silent for such a long moment that Longarm was about to ask her to get started, then she said slowly, "This man you have come to find, I think I might know more about him than I could say while the agent was listening."

Longarm's years of questioning suspects and others involved in criminal activity brought out his next question almost instinctively. He asked, "Because you was afraid it'd get you in trouble?"

"Not me alone," she replied slowly. "My brother Tonesco, and maybe my father and mother as well."

"Well, suppose you just start from the first and tell me what's bothering you," Longarm suggested.

"It was more than two weeks ago when my brother came to me," Se-Na-Ha began hesitantly. "He was afraid. He wanted to know what to do."

"To do about what?"

"Tonesco was coming home across the lava bed when he found it," she went on, obviously choosing her words carefully. "He had gotten to the big spring that comes up near the

41

forks of the Rio Blanco when he found..." She fell silent again.

"What'd he find?" Longarm prompted her.

"A dead man lying beside the water. Not one of our people, but a white man. The man had been shot."

Chapter 5

"Where was this body?" Longarm prodded. "And what'd the fellow look like when he was alive?"

"Tonesco did not tell me very much," Se-Na-Ha replied. "Only that he found the man's body lying by the water."

"What'd this dead man look like?" Longarm asked for the second time.

"Tonesco did not say. Just that the man was close to the spring and that he was dead."

"Had he been shot in the head, or the heart?"

Again Se-Na-Ha shook her head. "This I do not know. I do not remember Tonesco saying anything except that he could tell the dead man had been killed with a gun."

"Now, look here, Se-Na-Ha, your brother must've said a lot more'n you've told me about. I want you to think back and tell me just as near as you can everything that you can remember him telling you."

Somewhere in the house a clock began chiming the hour.

Its muffled note rang out four times and then was quiet. Se-Na-Ha remained silent until the clear small chimes stopped echoing. Then she sighed and began, "Tonesco was going to stop at the spring to drink and to water his horse. He was coming back from hunting, and it was already growing dark. He did not see the dead man until he had gotten off his horse and gone up to the spring. Then he did not know what to do."

"Four o'clock," Longarm said. "Where's you brother now? Over at the house where you stay?"

"No. I told him to go home. My family's house is three hours' ride from here. I thought that if Tonesco got home before our parents were awake, he could tell them that he got back soon after they had gone to bed."

"Why'd you tell him to do that?" Longarm frowned. "Did you figure maybe he had a fight and killed that fellow, instead of just stumbling onto his body?"

"Tonesco would not kill a stranger!" Se-Na-Ha protested. She was silent for a moment, then went on, "I do not know why I told him to go home. It seemed a good thing for him to do then, but maybe it was not."

"You ain't talked to him since, I guess?"

"No. I told Tonesco to stay with our family for two or three days, then go to the west to visit our older brother. His house is on the Mancos River, a full day's ride from where our parents live."

Se-Na-Ha fell silent. Longarm waited for a moment, then prodded her to go on with her story. "Well, let's go back over what happened. Your brother saw this body, and then what'd he do?"

"He told me he did nothing for a while, just stood looking at the dead man and trying to decide what he should do. After a while he grew afraid. He thought that someone who knew he had passed over the trail might tell the white police that he had been there. Then he might be accused of the killing. He pulled the body away from the spring and hid it in a gully close by."

"Why in tunket did your brother do a thing like that?" Longarm frowned. "All he had to do was skedaddle and nobody would ever have known he'd been there."

"This is what I told him," Se-Na-Ha said. "And Tonesco

44

said he did not stop to think, or he would not have moved the dead man."

"Which way is that spring from here?"

"North. Six miles, maybe eight."

"You think you can find it in the dark?"

"Of course. It is just beside the trail, and I have gone over the trail many times since I was a child."

"I guess there's a spare horse around here you can ride?"

"Of course. Why do you—" Se-Na-Ha stopped short for a moment, then went on, "Do you want me to show you where the spring is?"

"That's what I got in mind," Longarm replied. "If that dead man is the deputy I'm looking for or the fellow he was trailing, I got to know about it right quick."

"What will the agent say if I am not here and he does not know where I have gone?"

"I sure ain't going to leave without telling him," Longarm told her. "But that don't mean I got to explain anything to him. And likely he'll be too sleepy to ask a lot of questions. Don't you worry about that part. You just show me which room is his, and I'll take care of the rest."

"I will show you, of course. It is just down the hall from here."

"If that's the case, you don't need to show me. Just tell me how many doors to pass before I knock."

"There are two doors before the stairway and one more after you pass it. The next door is the agent's room."

"You wait while I get my duds on, then I'll go tell him."

Longarm dressed hurriedly in the dark. By now his eyes had grown accustomed to the almost total obscurity, and he moved swiftly as he pulled on his trousers and shirt, slid his feet into his boots, and buckled on his gunbelt. Lifting his vest off the chair-back, he went out into the hall. The starglow of the night sky coming through the wide windows made the corridor seem light in comparison to the darkness of his room. He stopped at the door Se-Na-Ha had told him to, and tapped lightly. Half a minute passed before Collins answered in a voice muffled with sleep.

"Who is it?"

"Custis Long, Mr. Collins."

"Is something wrong?" the Indian agent asked.

Without deviating from the literal truth, Longarm replied, "Not a thing, except I woke up sudden-like a while back, and before I could go back to sleep I got a hunch I need to do some backtracking over a stretch of that country I crossed today. By the time I get to where I'm heading it'll be full daylight, but I need somebody to show me the way so I don't get off on a false trail in the dark. I figured maybe you wouldn't mind if I take that Ute girl I talked to right after I got here. She'd be a likely one to guide me. She seemed right smart."

"Se-Na-Ha?" Collins asked.

Longarm could visualize the Indian agent's puzzled-frown by the tone of his voice.

"That's her. I don't figure to be gone much past noon."

After a lengthy wait, Collins replied. His voice still fogged with sleep, he said, "Do you know where to find her?"

"There ain't any place she could be except in one of them houses out back of here," Longarm answered. "I'll find her, all right."

"I don't quite understand what this is all about," Collins answered. "But you struck me as a man who knows what he's doing and gets a little impatient if he has to wait before he acts on his hunches. If Se-Na-Ha agrees to guide you, I haven't any objections."

"I'm mighty obliged to you, Mr. Collins," Longarm said. "Look for me back in time for supper, unless I've hit on a trail I need to follow. If I do, I'll send the girl back soon as I make up my mind."

Without waiting for the Indian agent to reply, Longarm walked back to his own room.

"We can go soon as we get saddled up," he told Se-Na-Ha. "I still don't know the lay of the land around this place. You'll have to show me where the horse corral is."

"It is only a few steps," she said. "Come with me." Longarm picked up his rifle and followed her to the stairs. As they descended and went outside she went on, "The corral is be-

46

hind the house where I stay and the ones where the two reservation policemen live with their wives."

Longarm frowned. "Why didn't you go tell your own policemen what you told me?"

"I said nothing because the men here are not friendly with my family. Besides, both of them are out on patrol. That is one reason why I worry, that one of them will find the body Tonesco hid and perhaps accuse him of killing the man."

"Why'd they do a thing like that?"

"You do not know our tribe well, do you, Marshal Long?"

"Far as I can recall, I only had a case or two where there was Utes mixed up."

"We are a quarrelsome people," Se-Na-Ha said. "In the old days, we fought among ourselves more often than we did against other tribes, or against the whites who were coming into our lands. Our old men say that is why you defeated us so easily."

They had reached the corral now, and their eyes had become adapted to the starlit darkness. Longarm's saddle was resting on one of the enclosure's horizontal fence rails, and he busied himself saddling up.

Se-Na-Ha threw a folded blanket over the back of one of the other horses and pushed a bit that was more like a hackamore than a bridle on its head. She stood waiting, watching Longarm as he finished saddling the livery horse. When she saw he had finished, she swung up on the back of the animal she had selected. As soon as Longarm was in his own saddle, she led the way from the corral toward the lava-covered *malpais*.

They moved through the starlit darkness. The only noise that broke the pre-dawn stillness was that of their horses' hooves, first thudding dully on the island of hard earth that surrounded the reservation headquarters, then grating and cracking when they started across the lava-covered *malpais*. Longarm kept the head of his mount even with the cruppers of the Indian pony Se-Na-Ha had chosen, and let her set the pace.

While they rode, the eastern horizon began to show streaks of dull red, which faded to pink, then the pink was washed from the sky by the white-gold hue of sunrise and above them the dark blue of night was banished by the brilliance of a new day.

"How much further we got to ride?" Longarm asked as he pulled the brim of his new Stetson lower to shield his eyes.

"Not far." Se-Na-Ha pointed ahead. "You can see where the grass grows around the spring now."

Longarm squinted into the sun-bright landscape and found the barely visible line of green. He nodded and nudged the livery horse to a faster walk. As the sky grew brighter, he could see the trail that led to the green oasis, a narrow winding strip where the surface had been disturbed by the hooves of horses. Another quarter of an hour brought them to the grass-covered island of green, an oasis alien to its lava-layered surroundings. The spring rose in the center of the green patch, its water trickling in two or three finger-wide channels until it reached the lava and vanished.

Swinging from his saddle, Longarm looked around at the featureless surface of the reddish-brown lava that surrounded them on all sides.

"I don't guess you got any idea where your brother hid that body?" he asked.

Se-Na-Ha shook her head. "No. But it cannot be far."

"Let's find it, then," he said. "You go that way, and I'll look on the other side."

They separated and began picking their way over the shifting chunks of porous stone, moving slowly, scanning the ground for signs that it had been disturbed recently. It was Longarm who saw the improvised grave, a rectangle in a little depression where the texture of the lava's surface showed that it had been disturbed recently.

He called to Se-Na-Ha, "Looks to me like I've spotted the grave. I'll dig into it. You don't have to help if seeing a dead man's going to spook you."

"I have seen dead men before," she replied calmly as she started toward Longarm.

For a moment he watched her as she picked her way across the treacherous footing. Then he hunkered down and began throwing aside the chunks of recently disturbed lava rock. It

48

was porous and very light, and Longarm had moved a good portion of it even before Se-Na-Ha joined her efforts with his. Within a very few minutes they had cleared a wide swath of the loosely piled lava and could see the fabric of a covert-cloth garment through the cracks in the cover.

"There's somebody buried here, that's for sure," Longarm said. "And I sure hope it ain't who I think it is."

They kept working until they had uncovered the head and shoulders of a man who'd been buried face down in the lava. Longarm scooped away the porous chunks to free the corpse's head and managed to turn it sideways.

Even before he could get a glimpse of the dead man's face, he saw the scarred cheek which told him the body was that of the Fort Smith deputy marshal. When he'd turned the limp head another inch or two, he saw the red X that had been smeared on the dead man's forehead, the mark of Gunge Peyton.

"It's Jim Houlihan, all right," he told Se-Na-Ha.

"Then we do not need to look further," she said. She stopped tossing the chunks of lava aside and hunkered back on her heels. "He is dead. We can do nothing to change that."

Houlihan was far from being the first fellow lawman whom Longarm had seen die violently. He had learned long ago to control his anger with the killer as well as to avoid showing any sorrow or grief he might feel. No emotion showed on his face or crept into his voice when he spoke.

"I got to go through his pockets to see if there's anything in 'em that'd give me a clue to where he was heading, because I already know who killed him."

"How do you know that?" Se-Na-Ha frowned.

Longarm pointed to the bloody X on the murdered deputy's forehead and explained, "I know the name of the man Jim was trailing. Gunge Peyton. Jim must've been closing in on him, so Peyton ain't too far ahead."

"And you will follow him, then?"

"I been following him all along. But I got to see that Jim gets buried before I start looking for Peyton, so I'm going to ask you to help me lug him in to the Indian Agency and see if your boss will mind having him buried decent there."

Se-Na-Ha nodded and silently went back to removing the rest of the lava stones. Longarm joined her, and within a few minutes they were able to lift the limp corpse from its crude grave. Longarm began searching the dead man's pockets, but found them empty.

"Whoever killed Jim taken everything he had," he said. "and sure as God made little green apples it was Gunge Peyton that shot him. Jim likely caught up with him here, and I guess Peyton seen him coming across this bare ground."

Se-Na-Ha had worked in silence while they were removing the lava rock from the improvised grave. Now she said, "If you do not mind riding double, I will ride with you and we can put your friend's body across my pony to carry him back to the agency."

"That'll be just fine, Se-Na-Ha," Longarm nodded. "Now we got him uncovered, we might as well load him on."

"I will lead the pony down here," she said, turning to start toward the tethered horses.

Longarm lighted a cigar while he stood staring down at Jim Houlihan's body. Except for a small black-rimmed hole left by the murderer's bullet, which had gone through the left pocket of the dead deputy's shirt, he might have been sleeping. Longarm was still standing looking at the corpse, restraining a fresh surge of anger, when Se-Na-Ha returned leading her pony.

"You ever handled a body before?" Longarm asked her.

"Yes, of course. The women of our people always prepare the bodies of our dead for the men to bury. Don't worry, Marshal Long. I will not be afraid."

"I wasn't thinking about that, Se-Na-Ha," Longarm told her. "But if you never loaded a corpse on a horse, I was—"

"I know what to do," she broke in. "We must both lift him by his arms and place him against the side of the horse. Then one of us must take his legs and the other lift his shoulders to get him on the pony's back."

"That's just about what I was getting at," Longarm said. "So if you're ready, let's get it over with."

With Se-Na-Ha on one side of the dead man and Longarm on the other, they lifted Houlihan's limp form and got the arms across the pony's back. The period of rigor mortis, when the body stiffened into an unmanageable rigidity, had passed long ago, and the dead man's form slumped down, his knees bending as the body sagged.

"He ain't going to stay if we don't keep hold of him," Longarm warned Se-Na-Ha. "I done this before, so I know how it is. You go over to the other side of the horse while I hold him, then take his wrists and pull while I lift up his feet and push."

He held the limp form in place while Se-Na-Ha went to the other side of the pony and grasped the dead man's forearms. Then Longarm moved behind the sagging body and bent down to take hold of the ankles. He could not close his hands over the corpse's booted ankles to grip them, so he worked the boots off the dead man's feet. Then he grabbed the body's ankles and boosted while Se-Na-Ha tugged, and between them they got Houlihan's limp form draped over the pony's back.

Longarm bent down and picked up the boots he'd taken off the dead man. As he straightened up, holding them by the heels, a small, square leather packet slipped out of one boot and dropped on the lava rocks with a dull metallic thud. Frowning, Longarm picked up the small object. It was unusually heavy, and his frown changed to a look of puzzlement when he lifted out the packet's contents and found himself holding a shining new twenty-dollar gold piece.

Se-Na-Ha came around the rump of her pony. She said, "If we're ready to start, I'll get on your horse and—" She saw Longarm examining the coin and broke off to ask, "What is that you've found?"

"Money," Longarm replied, holding up the golden disc for her to look at. "A double-eagle. It dropped outa one of Jim's boots when I picked 'em up."

"It is very pretty," Se-Na-Ha said. "I have never see one before. But why do you call it a double-eagle?"

"Why, I can't rightly tell you, Se-Na-Ha. Ever since I remember, a twenty-dollar gold piece has been called that."

"This gold piece is worth twenty silver dollars?"

"That's right."

"A silver dollar I know about," Se-Na-Ha went on. "My people value them greatly. But for this one coin to be worth so much . . ." She shook her head and asked, "Can I hold it and look at it closer?"

"Why, sure."

Longarm handed her the coin. She examined it carefully on both sides, then looked for a second time at the Liberty head and asked, "Is the lady on it someone real?"

"For all I know, she could be. But it seems like she's supposed to look like the head of that big statue they're talking about putting up back east, in New York, if they can ever get around to it. They call it the Statue of Liberty."

"Of this I have never heard." The Ute girl frowned. "But why would your friend have been carrying it in his boot?"

"That's what I been asking myself ever since I seen it," Longarm replied. "Maybe it was money he was keeping back in case he got in a tight spot, but a boot'd seem to me to be a mighty uncomfortable place to carry something as big as this."

Se-Na-Ha was looking at the gold piece again. She raised her head and asked, "Why is there a snake on it? It does not go well with such a pretty-faced lady."

"Snake?" Longarm frowned. "Where'd you see a snake? I sure didn't notice one."

"Here, on the other side from the face of the lady," she told him, holding the coin out for him to examine. "And across from the snake there is a number, three."

Longarm took the double-eagle from her and scrutinized it closely. The engraving on the reverse side of the gold piece was so tiny as to be almost invisible, but just as Se-Na-Ha had said, there was the coiled snake and a tiny "3" on the coin's obverse, in the small bare vees formed by the outspread wings and tail of the eagle.

"Well, I sure don't know a whole lot about things like this," Longarm said. "But this ain't no time for us to be figuring out puzzles, Se-Na-Ha. If we don't get started back to the agency, there won't be time to get poor old Jim Houlihan buried before dark. I'll tuck this coin away and see what I can find out about it later."

Chapter 6

"Looks like I'm going to be hitting the trail again first thing in the morning," Longarm told Cameron Collins as they sat at the table over coffee after dinner. Se-Na-Ha was clearing away the supper plates and dishes, carrying them to the kitchen, then returning for a fresh load.

"I'll hate to see you go," the Indian agent said. "There's so little to do around here most of the time that a visitor's always welcome. I'm just sorry that finding the body of your friend made your visit here a sad one."

"A man gets used to things like that in the work I do," Longarm replied. "And I ain't much on going to church. But I don't think there's a preacher anyplace that could've said a better prayer over poor Jim Houlihan than you did when we buried him this evening."

"I was glad I could help," Collins said, then asked, "Do you think you'll be able to find the man who killed him?"

"I don't aim to give up trying, even if all I got now is a

busted trail. Jim must've had a pretty good idea where Gunge Peyton was heading for, because he didn't lallygag around in Alamosa, he just pushed on through, heading west."

"Then you'll have to backtrack, won't you?"

"Looks like it," Longarm nodded. "I ain't got no more idea than Adam's off-ox where Houlihan picked up Peyton's trail, but that's sure to be what taken him to Alamosa. All I'm sure about is that someplace along the line he dug up something that started him this way."

"But you don't know where that someplace is, or what kind of clue he ran across," the Indian agent said thoughtfully.

"You're right about that. But I'll be leaving with more'n I had when I come here. If I can figure out what that double-eagle I found in Jim's boot meant, it might turn out to be a real help tracking Peyton."

"You didn't mention finding anything when you and Se-Na-Ha brought your friend's body in," Collins said.

"I was thinking more about getting him buried than anything else," Longarm said. He dug into his pocket and took out the gold piece, slid it from its leather container, and handed it to Collins. "You got to look pretty close to see where it's been marked."

Collins studied the coin for a moment, holding it close to the coal-oil lamp that occupied the center of the table. After a moment of squinting scrutiny he laid the coin on the table, stood up, and said, "Excuse me a minute, Marshal Long. These marks are too small to be very plain, but I have a reading glass in the office that will bring them up."

Se-Na-Ha returned to the room a moment after Collins had left. She said, "I heard what you said to the agent. Tonight I will pack some food for you to take. It might be a long ride that you are starting on."

"Well, that's right nice of you," Longarm told her. "I got some jerky and parched corn in my saddlebags, but real grub sure tastes a lot better."

Before Se-Na-Ha could answer, Collins returned. She picked up the remaining dishes and returned to the kitchen. The Indian agent put the large magnifying glass he was carrying on the table and slid the lamp to a spot in front of his chair, then sat down and picked up the gold piece. Holding it close to the lamp and peering at it through the powerful magnifier, he studied the coin for a few moments, both the obverse and reverse. Frowning thoughtfully, he looked across the table at Longarm.

"This snake and the number weren't just scratched on here by some amateur using the point of a knife," he announced. "It's a very skillful engraving job, done with professional tools."

"Well, whoever done it's breaking a law, then," Longarm said. "Nobody's supposed to mark up United States money, any more'n they are to counterfeit it. But I'd like to take a look at that coin through your magnifying glass."

Collins passed the gold piece and magnifier over to him, and Longarm studied the engraving that had been added to the obverse side of the coin. After he'd examined it thoroughly, he handed the glass back to Collins and, after sliding it back into its container, tucked it back in his pocket.

"I got a hunch this double-eagle means trouble," he said. "It's tied into this case I'm on right now, I'm dead sure of that, so I'll hang onto it till I close my case and get back to Denver. If I ain't found out what them signs on the back mean, I'll pass it over to the Secret Service men at the branch Mint there. It ain't but a step across the street from the office I work out of."

"My guess is that the gold piece is some kind of identification for a gang of criminals," Collins suggested.

"That's the way I figure," Longarm nodded. "And I might run into a time when I'll need it, seeing as how Jim Houlihan had it hid in his boot." He stood up and extended his hand to the Indian agent, saying, "I'll thank you for your help and bid you goodbye tonight, Mr. Collins. I'm going to be riding out before daybreak tomorrow, because I ain't got no time to waste."

"It's too bad you can't stay longer," Collins said. "You certainly will be welcome if you pass this way again. We have too few visitors in this isolated spot."

"It ain't likely I'll be back, not unless I get led around in some kind of a circle," Longarm replied. "But I thank you for the invite. Now, I guess I better get upstairs to bed. Daylight'll be along before we know it."

Longarm had just crawled into bed after blowing out the lamp on his bedside table. The desert night was warm, and he'd tossed aside even the thin Chimayo blanket and the top bedsheet before lying down. His eyes hadn't yet adjusted to the room's sudden and almost total darkness when a feather-light tapping on the door broke the silence.

"Who is it?" he called.

"Is me, Se-Na-Ha. I have brought you food for tomorrow."

"Come on in, then. I've already blowed the lamp out, but it won't be no trouble to light it again."

Longarm heard the click of the doorknob and a soft rustling of cloth as the Ute girl came into the room.

"I'll touch a match to the lamp," Longarm said, sitting up in the bed. "No use in you stubbing your toes on a chair or something."

"No. I do not need the lamplight," Se-Na-Ha replied. The latch clicked again as she closed the door. "I will put the food here on this chair by the door. There is fresh bread from supper and some pieces of cooked meat. It is not much, but it will keep you from being hungry if you do not stay too many days on the trail of the man who killed your friend."

"Thanks, Se-Na-Ha," Longarm said. "You sure been a help to me since I got here. I wish there was something I could do more'n saying thank you."

To his surprise the Ute girl replied, "There is."

"Well, now, I can't figure—"

She interrupted him. "I would like to share your bed with you tonight."

Longarm could make out Se-Na-Ha's shadowy figure standing at the foot of the bed by now. He could not see her clearly, only as the blurred shape of a darker hue than that of the room's whitewashed walls. He was silent for a moment, then he asked, "You sure that's what you want to do?"

"I am sure," she replied. "Since you got here I have wondered what it would be like to lie under you."

"I'll say one thing for you, Se-Na-Ha. You sure come right out and say what you want."

"I have been with men before, Longarm. I have had two husbands and sent both of them from my bed. But there are no men I care about here at the agency office, and I have not been able to go to one of our villages for many weeks."

"If you want to try me out, I sure ain't going to say no," Longarm told her. He was not greatly surprised by Se-Na-Ha's request, for in the past he'd encountered other Indian women who had been equally forthright. "Hop in and we'll get a lot better acquainted real sudden."

Longarm could glimpse Se-Na-Ha moving and hear the faint whisper of cloth against cloth. He began unbuttoning his longjohns to slip them off, but had gotten only to the middle button at the waist when the bed sagged on one side as Se-Na-Ha kneeled beside him.

She was now close enough for Longarm to see, even in the darkness. Her midnight-black hair blended with the surrounding gloom, but her features were outlined in the squared oval of her face, dark eyes above high cheekbones, full lips that were parted enough to show the gleam of her teeth above the blunted oval of her chin.

Se-Na-Ha's shoulders were wide, as wide as her hips. The rosettes of her small high breasts were a handspan apart. Her waist was barely indented above her hips, and her sturdy thighs were spread slightly apart.

"I will help you," she said, joining her hands with Longarm's in unbuttoning his undersuit.

Longarm dropped his shoulders back onto the mattress and raised his hips to let Se-Na-Ha strip the longjohns down and pull them free from his feet. His erection had begun, but was not yet full. Se-Na-Ha tossed the undersuit to the floor and closed one hand around his half-flaccid shaft.

"Ai-ee!" she said softly. "You are not yet ready for me. I will help you get ready, too."

She began opening and closing the hand that was fondling him with a slow deliberate rhythm to which Longarm responded almost at once. He began to swell, and Se-Na-Ha slowed the steady pulsing of her caresses. Longarm raised himself on an elbow and sought her small firm breasts with his free hand, but Se-Na-Ha pushed it down her body.

"Those are for tiny babies," she said. "Touch me in the place that is for a man."

Longarm let his hand drop and found the spot she had indicated. Se-Na-Ha was moist and ready, and the attention she'd been giving Longarm had brought him to a full erection. When his fingers touched her moist inner lips, she shuddered and freed his shaft, then used her hands to lever herself to the bed beside him.

When Longarm rose above her, she shifted her position to receive him, and Se-Na-Ha sighed, then gasped as he drove into her with a long deliberate thrust.

"Ai-ee!" she whispered. "You are bigger than my fingers told me!"

Longarm started stroking, a slow measured rhythm. Se-Na-Ha moaned softly and after a moment started squirming and sighing happily as she began to meet his strokes with upthrust hips. Longarm began driving harder and faster as she squirmed and sighed happily, then screamed softly and began trembling into her climax.

Se-Na-Ha clung to him, bucking and shuddering, and though Longarm slowed the tempo of his lunges he did not stop them completely. Even after she had sighed and her throaty cries subsided into breathy moans he continued to lunge slowly. For a moment Se-Na-Ha lay quietly, accepting his deep thrusting penetration, but she did not respond to his slowed rhythm.

After a few moments she asked in a whisper, "You can go on still longer?"

"Sure. I ain't got started good yet."

"Then do not stop. I have not found a man like you before. I am—" Her voice broke and almost at once began quivering again.

Longarm had pleased enough women to recognize the signal her body was giving him. He said nothing, but speeded up the rhythm of his lunges, shortening their tempo now, driving faster, until Se-Na-Ha was writhing beneath him, bucking her hips even more violently than before. He kept up the quickened stroking until once more her gasping breaths became short high-pitched cries, the sighs growing to moans and the moans transformed into throaty gasps of pleasure. Then she trembled again and writhed wildly before gasping loudly and going limp.

Even then he did not stop, but brought her to another peak. His body was sending him familiar signals now, but he maintained his long fast thrusts until Se-Na-Ha's soft cries again broke the silence of the quiet room. When he felt her hips rising he drove harder and faster again until he'd reached his own climax, then let himself relax on Se-Na-Ha's firm quivering form and lay quiescent while her rippling quivers died away and they both lay still, totally spent.

"You are much man," Se-Na-Ha said at last, breaking the silent darkness, her voice hoarse with repletion and exhaustion. "Never have I felt as I do now."

"I'm feeling pretty good myself," Longarm told her. "If you ain't in no hurry to leave, we can rest a while and maybe even doze a little bit before we have another go."

"You can do still more tonight?" she asked, her surprise apparent in the tone of her voice.

"Why, sure, if you feel like you want to."

"There is nothing I would like more. I did not know before that a man could give a woman such pleasure."

"I enjoyed giving you pleasure, Se-Na-Ha," Longarm assured her. "Now let's nap a little while before we start all over again."

Se-Na-Ha snuggled up to him with a satisfied sigh. Longarm stretched and yawned, suddenly sleepy. Then their eyes closed and the darkness was broken only by their soft, even breathing.

Though he'd been to Fort Smith before, Longarm saw as he gazed out the window that the town had changed a bit since his last visit. He stepped off the day coach of the St. Louis-Southwestern Railroad which had rattled his bones across Kansas over its rough new right-of-way from Wichita and walked with long strides along the tracks to the baggage car.

"I figured you'd be coming along real soon to pick up your

gear, Marshal Long, so I got it for you right here by the door," the baggage handler said when Longarm stuck his head inside the car's wide double side doors.

"Now, that's real thoughtful of you," Longarm said, reaching for his bedroll, saddlebags, and rifle as the man passed them down.

"I guess you remember how to get to the Federal Courthouse? There oughta be a hack outside the depot."

"I'll get there just as quick if I walk," Longarm said. "But thanks anyway, and thanks for taking care of my gear."

Tossing his bedroll over one shoulder, his saddlebags over the other, and balancing his rifle in one hand, Longarm walked in the warm sunshine from the depot to Rogers Avenue. There he turned up toward Third Street and the old fort that had been remodeled for use as the Federal Courthouse for the Arkansas District. The building was not large enough to confuse anyone. A wide main corridor led past the courtroom to Judge Isaac Parker's chambers and a light tap at the door brought Longarm an invitation to step inside.

"Well, Marshal Long," Judge Parker said as he looked up from his desk. His voice was light, but even during the few years since Longarm had last seen him, the man famous now as the "Hanging Judge" had aged. His hair was beginning to gray at the temples, though this sign of age and stress had not crept into his brown vandyke beard. The judge went on, "You certainly took your time getting here. I got the telegram you sent from Trinidad three days ago."

"Trinidad's a pretty far piece from here, Judge," Longarm replied. There was no strain of apology in his voice, and he was studying the jurist as he spoke. "Maybe you don't know it, but this is a real hard town to get to from where I was. I spent all three of them days on one train or another, and it feels good just to be getting my feet on the ground again."

"Well, now that you're here, tell me what you've found out about my deputy. I suppose you must have run across something, but there was no hint of it in your telegram."

"I figured it'd be better to wait till I could tell you face to face," Longarm said. "Jim Houlihan's dead. That murdering son of a bitch you sent him to bring in ambushed him out on the edge of Utah Territory and left him for buzzard meat."

After he'd sat silently for a moment, Judge Parker told Longarm, "I hope you're not through talking. I want to hear you say that you caught up with Gunge Peyton and brought him back here. I want him to go to the gallows where he was supposed to swing more than a month ago."

Longarm shook his head. "I ain't had time to run him to earth yet, Judge."

"Don't tell me he slipped away from you!"

"No, sir. But I was on his trail when I come across Jim Houlihan's body, and I ain't picked it up again yet."

"Then what the devil are you doing here in Fort Smith?" Parker demanded, his dark eyes snapping. "You didn't have to traipse all the way back here to report Houlihan's death. A telegram would've been faster and wouldn't've taken you off Peyton's trail!"

"That's what I'm trying to tell you, Your Honor. Peyton must've killed Jim two or three weeks before I even got on the case. After he done the murder, he just went on to wherever he was heading."

"And if you'd done your job, you'd be going right on after him this minute!"

"That ain't the way it is, Judge. Jim Houlihan had picked up Peyton's tracks someplace back here where there's folks that's seen him and saloons where a barkeep will remember him and where there's girls he might've laid up with and stores where he's bought grub, things like that."

"What you're telling me, then, is that Peyton's gotten away from you," Parker frowned.

"He has for right now," Longarm agreed. "But it won't be that way for long. On that Ute reservation there ain't no towns, and not too many people. There wasn't no way at all I could pick up a trace of Peyton. That's why I come back here, to dig up the places Jim went to. If he could pick up Gunge Peyton's tracks, so can I, but I got to start here and follow Jim Houlihan's trail till I get to where he learned the place Peyton was heading."

Parker nodded slowly, his brows pulled together, then told Longarm, "I see the point you're making, and I have to agree with you. You used good judgment, Marshal Long. Now tell me what I can do to help you. You didn't come in here just to pass the time of day. Whatever you want, I'll see that you get it, because I don't want to waste a moment getting you back on the trail of that man who killed my deputy."

"Mainly what I'd like to look at now is Jim Houlihan's reports," Longarm said. "I recall Jim telling me how you was about him sending a report every day when he was away from here on a case, even when he didn't do much of anything."

"Of course I do," Parker agreed. "I don't allow my men to loaf on the job, Long. Even if I might not read one of their daily reports until a week after I get it, George Maledon goes over them every day and gives me the important facts in them."

"I guess I better talk to him, then. If I read every word of what Jim sent in before he was killed, I might spot something."

"You'll remember where to find him," Parker nodded. "Out in the shed next to the gallows."

"Sure," Longarm replied. "And after I talk to him, I'll let you know what I've turned up. Now, I know you got other work to do, so I'll get outa your way."

Chapter 7

George Maledon hadn't changed any more than had the judge, Longarm saw when he entered the tiny office only a few yards from the permanent gallows in what had once been the cavalry stables. At least a third of the floor was covered with stacked coils of heavy manila rope. An ancient tottering table piled high with sheafs of paper took up most of the remaining floor space.

Maledon sat in a high-backed armchair in front of the table. He had on the same rusty black suit he'd been wearing the last time Longarm had seen him. Belted around his waist outside the coat in crossdraw holsters were the ivory-handled revolvers he favored. His hat was a Dakota-style Stetson, once creamy white but now dented and battered, its crown discolored and its wide brim warped into ripples. His opaque black eyes were fixed on Longarm, and between his small straggly moustache and the flared-out, whitening beard that reached halfway to his waist, his lips were curled in a smile of welcome.

"Howdy, Longarm," he said. "I wasn't looking to see you this far from Denver, but I guess you've come to talk about Jim Houlihan turning up missing over in your jurisdiction."

"He ain't missing any longer," Longarm replied. "Jim's dead. Shot. I buried him right by the Indian Agency office over on the Ute reservation just up from the border of New Mexico Territory."

"And you brought in the man that killed him, I suppose?" Maledon asked.

Longarm shook his head. "He was gone a long time before I found Jim's body. But I know who he is. He's one of your customers that got away from the pen before the time came for you to fit him with a rope."

"You'd be talking about Gunge Peyton, then," Maledon nodded. "He's the only one that's made a jailbreak and gotten away from me these past six years."

"It was Peyton that killed Jim, all right. I wasn't there when he done it, but Jim wasn't after nobody but Gunge. There wasn't anybody else around the place where Jim was gunned down that'd even know he was a deputy marshal, let alone shoot him."

"Where'd this happen?"

"About as far from anywhere as you could find. A place on the Ute Indian reservation that they call the Four Corners because it's where Mormon Territory and Arizona Territory and New Mexico Territory and Colorado all come together."

"I guess you're having to backtrack now because you got there too late to pick up Gunge Peyton's trail?" Maledon asked.

Longarm nodded. "You know as well as I do that you got to have some idea which way to go when you're backtracking. The only way I could see to get a line on where Jim might've been heading was to start from here and ask questions everyplace he went to. Someplace along the way, I'll find out where he was heading for, and that's what I need to pick up Gunge Peyton's tracks, too."

Maledon nodded. "I had to do that more than once or twice

myself when I was working over in the Indian Nation. Got so tired of moving around I was glad to say yes when the Judge wanted to know if I had any objections to taking charge of the gallows."

"Well, it ain't a job I'd care for, but like the old man said when he kissed the cow, everybody to his own tastes," Longarm replied. "But what I come to Fort Smith for is to get some idea where Jim has been. The judge said you'd have whatever reports he sent back here."

"There wasn't much in them, as I recall," Maledon said. "Jim was gone a long time, but I only got two reports from him."

"Either one of 'em might be the one I need. You mind digging 'em out?"

Maledon leaned back in his chair and began shuffling through one of the stacks of papers on the table. As his fingers riffled them, he said, "Jim must've been out of pocket two or three weeks before the judge begun fretting. Every day he'd ask me if I'd got a report from him, and every day I'd tell him no, but he didn't start worrying right away. Then he had to do a lot of telegraphing back and forth to Washington before he got the high muckety-mucks there to have Billy Vail put you on Jim's trail."

"All Billy could give me about those reports was that one come from Tonkawa, over in the Indian Nation, and the other one from Tascosa, up in the Texas Panhandle," Longarm said.

"How'd you happen to go to the Ute country, then?" Maledon frowned as he extracted two sheets of paper from the stack he was searching through and handed them to Longarm.

Longarm answered while he was scanning the reports Maledon had given him. "Jim wrote out a travel voucher at Trinidad when he headed for Alamosa. That was the last place where he left any sign he'd passed through. I trailed him sorta by guess and by God from Alamosa to where we dug him up on the Ute reservation."

"So now you've got to figure out where he'd been in between times," the hangman nodded.

"That's about the size of it," Longarm agreed. "And I got something else to find out about." He dug into his pocket, took out the small pouch, and extracted the twenty-dollar gold piece. Handing it to Maledon, he went on, "Jim's pockets was plumb cleaned out, but this was in one of his boots. See what you make of it while I read these reports."

Maledon took the coin and began examining it as Longarm started reading. He examined the obverse closely, turned the double-eagle over in his fingers to scrutinize the reverse, then took a second look at the Liberty head side. He held the gold piece in the palm of his hand, testing its weight. Then he went back to the reverse side for a second look.

In the meantime, Longarm was skimming quickly through the two reports. Both were short and very similar in wording. Jim Houlihan's big schoolboy-style writing was easy to read, but the reports told him nothing that he hadn't known before, except that the dead deputy had gone by longboat to Tonkawa, where Gunge Peyton had been arrested originally for the murder of an Indian Nation policeman.

No one Houlihan had questioned in the little town admitted to having seen Peyton there after his escape, though all of the men he'd talked to said they'd heard that the fugitive had passed through the town. Some of them were sure that Peyton was going to Dodge City, others put his destination as Tascosa, but most of those the deputy interviewed had claimed to be totally ignorant of the wanted man's plans.

"Well, even if Gunge Peyton ain't in Tonkawa, at least I got a place to start from," Longarm told Maledon when he'd finished going through the reports. "Two places would be closer to the mark, I guess."

"Then you got what you came here for," Maledon said. "Even if you are a month or so behind him."

"Like I told the judge, I couldn't backtrack from Alamosa because I didn't have no idea where Jim had been. Now I at least got someplace to head for first. Tonkawa's on the way to Tascosa, so I'll stop there just in case. Then I'll move on according to what I find out along the trail and sooner or later I'll catch up with Peyton."

"We've both done enough trailing to know how to go about it," Maledon said. He held up the gold piece and went on, "I

66

don't guess I understand about this double-eagle you gave me to look at. Where does it fit into your case?"

"So far, I ain't been able to figure that out," Longarm admitted. "But I don't figure Jim Houlihan would've tucked it away so careful, in that pouch and hid in his boot like it was, unless it means something."

"Oh, I'll agree with you on that," Maledon nodded. "And if you had me look at it to give you my idea about it, I'd guess it's something like a password is to a secret society, or a uniform, or like the badge we carry. Something to be sure the man that has it belongs."

"Belongs to what?"

"Oh, the Freemasons or the Fenians or the Texas Rangers or anything else you'd care to name, up to and including the U. S. Marshal's force."

"I see what you're getting at," Longarm nodded, then confessed, "I never was much of a one to join something, George. Maybe that's why it didn't come to me all at once what them marks on that gold piece had to stand for."

A thoughtful frown had grown on Maledon's face. Now he went on, "If the outlaws are getting formed up into a club where one of them helps the others when they're on the run or in a tight, we could be looking at a lot of trouble."

"I guess we could, at that," Longarm nodded. "But we've been up against gangs before. This one ought not to be much different. All of 'em overplays their hands, and winds up dead or behind bars."

Maledon handed the double-eagle back to Longarm. "You'd better keep this," he said. "If Jim thought enough of it to hide it away, he must've figured he'd need to use it. The first chance I get, I'll tell the judge what I think's going on, and he might figure out some way to fight it."

"You do that," Longarm told him. "Now, I got what I come here for, so I better get back to work. Since you told me what you did about Jim going in a longboat over to Tonkawa, I guess I'll walk on over to the river and ask a few questions. It might even turn out that I'll try to do just what Jim Houlihan did when he left here to take out after Gunge Peyton."

Longarm walked slowly along the riverfront, surprised at the activity he was seeing. Since he'd last visited Fort Smith, the river traffic had increased greatly from the few shallow-draft steamers he'd seen on its waters only a few years earlier. The wharves now stretched for two miles or more along the low levee, and vessels of all kinds were crowded prow to stern along the piers.

There were several passenger sidewheelers, their cabins rising boxlike from the decks; a handful of tow-boats, small in size, but with sturdy rear paddlewheels, tugging an uncountable number of scows and barges and flatboats, some empty, some piled high with cargo bound upriver or down. John-boats, their triple or quadruple sets of oars dipping with slow rhythm into the water, plied between the bigger vessels, and closer to the shore there were rowboats and small sculls. Some of these had a cargo of bulging towsacks; others, managed by only one or two men with oars or sweeps or poles, carried passengers from the vessels to and from the riverbank.

In common with all waterfronts, this one at Fort Smith had its share of idlers. Some were obviously rivermen recovering from a hard night in the town's saloons or gambling houses. Others were job-seekers, easily identified by their busy moves from boat to boat as well as by their heavy jackets and knit wool caps. A good share of the men along the shore could be tagged at once as drifters and bums; others had the look of temporarily stranded passengers waiting to board one of the passenger vessels. Two or three of them had the look of hardcases.

Guided by the long years of experience that had given him a virtual sixth sense in such matters, Longarm selected one of the hardcases and walked up to him.

"If I was wanting to go upriver right away and on across the Indian Nation, what sorta boat would I be looking for?" he asked.

"That'd depend on how big a hurry you're in," the man replied, his eyes narrowing as he examined Longarm and noted the bulge of his Colt under his coat.

"Well, now, I ain't exactly running, but I been hearing

about that mean son of a bitch you got here, the one folks calls the Hanging Judge, and I figure the best thing I can do is move on," Longarm replied.

"If you wasn't in a hurry and was short of money, you'd be looking for a johnboat carrying cargo upriver," the man said. "Or if you need to get out fast, take a paddlewheeler upriver to where they ain't got enough draft, and you don't mind winding up in Texas, then get on one of the johnboats that's going up the Canadian. It'll get you close to the Texas line, but after that you'll have to hire a horse or go shank's mare."

What the stranger had said about going upstream on the Canadian River to Texas struck a responsive chord in Longarm's mind. Tascosa was the first town on his list to visit, and he'd been there before, knew that the Canadian River flowed just outside the town.

"You wouldn't happen to know where there's one of them johnboats going up the Canadian that's about ready to pull out?" Longarm asked. "I got a notion to shake this town's dust off my feet fast as I can. Texas sounds pretty good to me."

"Texas sounds to me like you're in some kind of trouble," the man said, cocking his head as he examined Longarm closely.

"Let's just say I'd like to get moving fast," Longarm told him. "I been hearing too much about that Hanging Judge here."

"I guess you've got travelling money?"

"All I figure I'll need."

"It'd be worth something to you if I put you next to a man that's getting ready to take a johnboat load up the Canadian, wouldn't it?"

Instead of answering with words, Longarm reached into his pocket and pulled out a fistful of money. Normally, he'd have fished around for small change in silver, but his fine-honed lawman's instinct was at work by now. It told him that a half-clandestine trip such as the riverfront shill was hinting about might be the answer to getting on the trail followed by a fugitive like Gunge Peyton and a locally knowledgeable lawman like Jim Houlihan, who had left Fort Smith trailing Peyton.

Opening his hand to reveal the coins it contained, Longarm

picked out two cartwheels. Before he could offer them to the waterfront bum, the other man shook his head.

"If you're real anxious to get outa Fort Smith, you'll have to do better than that," he said.

Longarm let the silver dollars clink back into his palm and picked up a half-eagle. This time, the man did not object, but took the five-dollar gold piece and motioned for Longarm to follow him.

As they walked along the levee that bordered the river-bank, Longarm noticed how the anchored vessels changed character. They passed large passenger steamboats and wide, shallow barges at first. Then the steamboats began to diminish in size and numbers and were replaced by strings of smaller barges. When the barges thinned out, sweepboats, flatboats, and a few johnboats replaced them for a stretch. Then the sweepboats and flatboats gradually grew fewer, and before they'd gotten to the end of the levee the bigger boats grew fewer and fewer until only johnboats were left, swinging at their moorings.

"How much further we got to go?" he asked the man who was walking a half-step ahead of him.

"Just a short piece. And, since we're doing business together, we might as well get acquainted. My name's Coaster."

Longarm shook his head. "Doing business is one thing, but trading names is something else. You can call me Smith or Jones or whatever you please. It won't make no difference in us doing business together, and I'll feel better about it."

"Whatever you say," Coaster shrugged. "But where we're going is right up ahead now, and I figured our business would go easier if I had a name to put on you."

Longarm nodded, but said nothing as he took his attention away from Coaster and began noting his surroundings. There were only a few scattered johnboats along the river now, and the trees and bushes were crowding closer to the bank. They reached a little creek trickling into the main stream, and Coaster led Longarm along its banks for a dozen yards. He stopped and indicated a shanty just ahead.

"Maybe I better go in by myself first," he suggested. "I

need to let my friends know it's me bringing you here and not the other way around."

"Go ahead," Longarm nodded. "I'll wait."

Standing alone on the bank of the creek, Longarm lighted a cigar as he studied the cabin. By its looks, it had been there for a long time. It was of board-and-batten construction, windowless, as far as he could see, its door opening only a few yards from the creek. The roof shingles were curled and cracked. Vines grew up the walls at the corners and blended the little dwelling into the green of the country behind and around it.

He'd been waiting for only half a dozen cigar puffs when Coaster reappeared. Without closing the door, he motioned for Longarm to join him.

Inside, the cabin looked even more ramshackle than it had when seen from the creekbank. It had only one window, and it was overgrown with vines, plunging the interior into a sort of perpetual twilight. Two cots stood along the back wall and two more occupied the end walls. Only those at the sides seemed to be in use.

Two men sat at a battered table in the center of the room. One was old enough to be wearing a furry gray beard; the other was a bit younger and was clean-shaven. Both wore the battered black-billed caps, high-necked sweaters, and canvas pants that were the marks of a riverman, and both looked at Longarm with closed, expressionless faces.

Finally the older of the men said, "Coaster tells me you want to go upriver on the Canadian with us."

"That'd depend on more'n one thing," Longarm replied. "I'd be more interested was I sure you'll be leaving right off, and the other one's how much you'll want to take me along."

"Well, there ain't much chance we'll get more cargo, but your fare'll make up the difference, so if we make a dicker we can shove off right away. We're all loaded and provisioned up, so I guess all we need to do is see if you can pay the fare."

"How much you asking?"

"Fifty."

Longarm shook his head. "That's a mite rich for my blood. I wasn't figuring on more'n twenty."

"Split the difference, then. Make it twenty-five," the boatman said.

"Now, that's a figure I can see," Longarm agreed. He dug into his expense money for the second time. Picking out a double-eagle and a half-eagle, he held up the coins. "Twenty-five it is. When do we start out?"

"Right away, if it suits you."

"I'll have to go back to town and get my rifle and bedroll and saddlebags," Longarm told him. "I'll give you five now to fix the deal, and the twenty before we start out."

His face still expressionless, the boatman nodded. "We just might need your rifle if we get as far as Comanche country. Go on after your gear, mister. We'll be ready to shove off the minute you get back."

Chapter 8

"Isn't it a little bit soon for you to be leaving?" Judge Parker asked after he'd heard Longarm's plan to start his backtracking effort at once. "You just got to town a few hours ago."

"Maybe it is a mite sudden, Judge, but Gunge Peyton ain't going to lallygag along, wherever he's headed."

"Don't you think you'd make better time taking a train to where you're going, instead of that riverboat you mentioned?"

"I won't say time ain't important," Longarm frowned. "But after all the trouble I had on that train trip I taken to get here, I figure I'll save time and maybe even find out a few things I didn't know about if I go back on this fellow's boat."

"You still think you can pick up Peyton's trail by backtracking him, do you?"

"Well, there sure ain't nothing certain about it, but even a man on the run's got to leave some kinda traces that he's passed through a place. I know where to start looking again,

73

after seeing them reports George showed me, so with any luck I oughta dig up what I need."

"I hope you'll have the luck you need, then," Parker said. "In any event, it's your case, and you've handled enough to be sure of what you're doing."

"Maybe I don't know for sure, but I got sense enough to change plans if this one don't work out. But I got to excuse myself now, judge. I'm running late, because it took me more time than I'd figured on to get my gear outa that hotel room I rented, so I better get along."

"Just remember to send your reports to George Maledon," the judge said. "I want to know what's going on, damn it!"

"I'll do the best I can, Your Honor," Longarm promised. "Tell George for me that I'll see him next trip I make here. Now, I got to get cracking before that boatman gets tired of waiting for me."

With his bedroll over one shoulder and his rifle and saddlebags forming a balanced load for each hand, Longarm retraced his steps along the Fort Smith wharves until he reached the shanty. The riverboat men were still waiting for him, hunkered down in front of the tumbledown shack, but the older man who was so obviously the boss was not in the best humor.

"You sure taken your time," he told Longarm grouchily, as he walked down to the creekside and pulled on the mooring-rope to bring the johnboat closer to shore. "We won't get to the mouth of the Canadian while it's still daylight tomorrow unless we push off right now."

"I'm here now, and I sure don't hanker to stay any longer than I got to," Longarm answered. "We can go whenever you say the word."

"Money's the word, mister. The only kinda business I do is cash on the line," the boatman said. "Let's have the rest of your fare."

Longarm dug into his expense allowance again and handed two ten-dollar gold pieces to the boatman. While the man was tucking the coins into his pocket, he looked from one of the rivermen to the other and said, "We got a good ways to go, and I sorta like to know who I'm travelling with. I don't recall hearing Coaster mention your names."

74

"That makes us even," the riverman answered. "I don't know who you are, either."

"Why, I'll answer to Custis if you call me that."

"I'm Blunt," the boatman said. Then he pointed to the second riverman and went on, "He's Studs. Now, don't get upset if he takes hold of your gear, it'll have to be stowed where it balances the rest of the load and won't shift if we hit rough water."

Longarm acknowledged the introductions with a nod while Studs was stepping into the boat. When he extended his hands, Longarm handed over his saddlebags and bedroll, but did not follow them with the rifle. He watched while Studs tucked his other belongings into crevices between the sail-cloth-covered bundles that made up the cargo, then turned his attention to the johnboat itself.

Like most others of its kind, the narrow vessel was between twenty and twenty-five feet long, six or seven feet wide in the middle. It had a high prow which slanted downward for a quarter of the boat's length, then leveled off and rose slightly again into a slightly arched stern. A stubby mast rose from the center, which was filled with the canvas-shrouded bundles of cargo, lashed in place to keep them from shifting. A truncated lug-sail drooped from the mast, hanging limp, a good part of its canvas bunched up on the cargo around the mast's base.

Tholes for oars or sweeps were pegged into each of the wide siderails fore and aft, and a sturdier set of tholes in the stern was provided for a steering-oar or sweep. Three wide plank-seats spanned the boat's bow, and there were two more such seats in the stern. All the wooden areas were covered with thickly coated varnish, which was badly chipped and needed to be renewed. A film of water glistened in the bottom for an inch or two on each side of the keel.

"You better get in behind the cargo," Blunt told Longarm. "I ain't said anything about it before, but when we hit fast water you'll have to give me a hand with the sweep."

"Now, that's a job I never taken on," Longarm frowned. "I ain't real sure about what you said, but if I guess right, it means I'm going to have to do some work."

"On a boat like this, everybody does some work, Custis. It's part of what you pay for passage."

"I don't recall you mentioned that when we was dickering over the fare. I don't know much about boats, and I don't mind saying so right out."

"You'll learn fast enough," the riverman promised. "There ain't a lot of current in this damn river, but there's a few deep spots where I can't pole, and we'll all have to pull an oar to get through 'em."

"Well, I guess I'll just have to do the best I can," Longarm shrugged.

"Sure," Blunt nodded, picking up a pole from the thwarts. While he was working the pole through the stern tholes and sliding it into the water, Studs pulled away the mooring-line and tossed it to the shore. Then he worked his way up toward Longarm and picked up a pole like the one Blunt was using in the stern. Between them, they pushed the boat out into the current, then hurriedly unshipped long, thin-bladed oars.

Both men began rowing, turning the boat upstream, and heading it into the current. Longarm watched for a moment, then sat down. The rivermen's efforts set the johnboat moving slowly upstream but they made little headway until Blunt poled close to shore. There he caught a cross-current which allowed the vessel to move a bit faster. Longarm made no move to join his efforts to theirs until they had covered perhaps a quarter of a mile Then Blunt nudged him with the toe of his boot.

"You see about how much headway we're making. If you're in a hurry to get where we're going, you'll pick up one of them oars and give us a hand."

"I told you I don't know nothing about boats," Longarm replied. "But I guess I can give it a try."

"Just watch Studs," Blunt said. "After a while you'll get the knack of timing your strokes. Soon as you do, I'll pick up the pole and push, and we'll move a lot faster."

Keeping his eye on Studs and trying to pick up his rhythm, Longarm soon found that if he used his back muscles instead of his biceps the job of rowing was much easier. After a quarter of an hour, Blunt shipped his oar and began poling, and the johnboat moved appreciably faster. They'd been travelling upstream, staying close to the bunk, for perhaps a half-hour without speaking when Blunt broke the silence.

"We'll be in the serpentine in a few more minutes," he said. "Then I'll go back to rowing and you can knock off."

"I don't know what you're talking about, but I'll be glad to lay this oar down," Longarm told the boatman.

"Soon as we've passed that first bend up ahead the riverbed zigzags all the way to where we head up the Canadian," Blunt explained. "It sets up a funny kind of current that us rivermen calls the serpentine."

Longarm shook his head and said, "You're talking your own kinda lingo now, and it ain't all that easy for me to keep up with you. Maybe you better explain so's I can understand you."

"You're bound to know we're heading upstream," Blunt told him. "Now, when we hit the zigzags, they sorta curve the current off one side of the river across to the other bank. It don't move fast up that other side, but a boat don't have to buck it so much. What I'll do is cross from one bank to the other one at the right time, and we'll move a lot faster with a lot less work. All you'll have to do is give us a hand while we're going through the eddies from one bank to the other one."

"I'll just take your word for it," Longarm told the boatman.

Slowly, the boat made its way upstream. Longarm tried to turn his head to look upriver, but found that he was unable to time his strokes, and soon gave up the effort. His first indication that they were in the eddies Blunt had tried to explain to him was when the riverman shipped his oar and took up the long pole again. Suddenly the water seemed to present less resistance to Longarm's oar, and the boat began moving a bit faster.

They reached a point where only a dozen yards separated them from the bank, and he heard the splashing of Studs's oar increase its tempo. The boat slowly swung to move parallel to the shore, and its speed again increased. Blunt put the pole down and went back to rowing. Longarm was trying to match his strokes when Blunt spoke again.

"You can ship your oar, Custis," he said. "Me and Studs will handle it from here till we get to the Canadian. But that won't be till late tomorrow, and you'll still have to pitch in to get us back and forth when we go from one bank to the other. Anyhow, you can rest a while."

Longarm shipped his oar and rubbed his palms together. In spite of their calluses, his hands felt like he'd been rubbing them over an especially coarse grindstone. He took a cigar from his pocket and lighted it while he watched the heavily forested shoreline slip past the boat.

"Well, I guess I'll last till we get where we're headed for," he said to Blunt. "But next time I got to make a trip like this one, I made up my mind I'll just stick to a horse."

"There ain't but one thing wrong with this damn river," Longarm remarked as he gazed at the high banks of reddish earth through which the johnboat was now moving slowly. "It's got too many twists and bends in it. Seems like it just can't make up its mind which way it wants to go."

"Why, we're making good time, Custis," Blunt said. "We only been travelling nine days."

"How many more days you figure it'll be before we hit the Texas line?"

"We're just about in spitting distance right now," the riverman replied. "If we can get over the shallows up ahead without grounding and push on for a while after dark, we can sleep in Texas tonight."

"Now, that's the best news I've had since we started out," Longarm observed. "I ain't trying to do you no favors, Blunt, but if it'll help us go faster, I'll pull an oar a while."

"I didn't aim to ask you to," Blunt said. "But now you've made the offer, I won't try to stop you. Grab hold of that one you always use and start pulling."

With Longarm's oar adding impetus to the johnboat's progress, they moved appreciably faster. The nine days he'd spent with the riverboat men had done little to make him feel at home with them. Blunt and Studs had kept to themselves. Neither had said a great deal to Longarm, other than to answer his questions. Their quick meals had been eaten in silence, and the hard work of pushing the poles and manning the oars had not encouraged either them or Longarm to waste breath on conversation.

Aside from their short overnight stops, pulling into the riverbank to sleep and eat, they'd made only one stop. This had been at a little settlement on the border between the Cherokee and Seminole reservations, where they'd bought parched corn, jerky, and a steer-gut filled with pemmican. For most of the time, the high banks of crumbling soil through which the Canadian flowed had cut them off from the lands bordering the stream as effectively as though they'd been in a railroad coach with its window blinds drawn, passing quickly from one tunnel to another.

Though he'd done very little travelling on johnboats, Longarm had been able to tell that they were making better progress now than had been the case at the start of their trip. Even during the early stage of their travel, soon after they'd left the Arkansas River and started up the Canadian, the current had diminished steadily, enabling them to move faster with less effort. Each day saw the river bottom shelving more and more, into long shallow stretches where the oar he manned when the stream was filled with cross-currents and eddies would scrape bottom frequently.

More obvious than the change in the character of the river's bed was the difference in its channel. In its lower winding stretches the Canadian had flowed through well defined banks that rose abruptly and towered high above the water's surface. Soon after their stop to replenish provisions, both the channel of the stream and the land through which it flowed took on a new appearance.

In the area they were traversing now, the banks no longer jutted up high and straight from the water's edge. Here, where the river's waters flowed brown instead of the red they'd been earlier, it ran between banks that rose only a few feet above the stream's rippling surface. Beyond these low banks the land sometimes stretched for half a mile or more and was covered with large jumbled patches of uprooted trees and bushes before the level area ended at the bottom of high bluffs that dropped almost vertically from the prairie.

"I'd sure hate to try to come up this river when it's as high as it looks like it gets," he remarked to Blunt as they were passing such a stretch of devastation. "You ever see it when it's flooded?"

"Sure," the boatman replied. "Why, a time or two I been here there'd be a regular wall of water twenty or thirty feet high and all full of brush and trees come rushing at the boat."

"What do you do if you get caught like that?"

"Pull to shore fast as you can and run like hell and hope you make it to the high ground before the water hits you."

"What about your boat, and your cargo?"

"Oh, we might lose some of our load if it ain't been lashed down real good. And the boat'll get stove-in, more or less. But all you can do is wait till the water drops and walk downriver till you find where the boat's shoaled. Then you fix it up and start moving again."

"Well, I'll tell you something," Longarm said with a thoughtful frown. "There's times when I been out on the prairie and up in the high country when a winter storm comes along, and they ain't real nice to fight through. But, for my part, I'll stick to a horse and ride. A boat makes a man do too much work."

Before Blunt could answer, the boat lurched and stopped and started to swing in the current. He grabbed his pole and, after a bit of hard heaving and pushing, helped by the similar efforts Studs was making in the prow, freed the craft from the river bottom and had it moving upstream again.

"We're getting to shallow water, ain't we?" Longarm asked.

"It's been shoaling up for quite a while now, in case you ain't noticed," Blunt told him.

"How much further you figure we can go?"

"I ain't real sure we can get as far as the Texas line," the boatman frowned. He glanced at the sky. The sun was already well down toward the horizon and was beginning to take on its reddish sunset hue. "But I ain't giving up yet. We'll push on till it gets too dark to see, and take a good look at the water in the morning. Maybe it'll be deep enough for us to get a few miles further on."

Until the sun had set and the twilight deepened so that the bluffs through which the riverbed wound were almost invisible, the boatmen kept the johnboat moving. The keel scraped bottom a time or two, but when Longarm added his strength with a third push-pole, they managed to get the craft moving again. At last the light failed completely, and Blunt called to Studs.

"Let's call it a day," he said. "We're liable to get in trouble if we keep on pushing. We're inside of a half-day from the Texas line, and if we get lucky we'll be able to make it the rest of the way when we can see to read the water."

With the boat shored and tethered, they ate a cold meal and turned in. The sky was just beginning to fade in the east when the thudding of Blunt's boots on the bottom of the johnboat echoed in Longarm's ears and brought him instantly awake. He sat up, pushed his blankets aside, and got to his feet. In the prow he saw Studs rising from his bedding.

"Let's give it a try," Blunt said. He'd already started chewing a strip of jerky. "Once we get another two or three miles, we'll hit a long stretch of good water. If we're lucky, we'll make it all the way."

"Start whenever you're ready," Longarm told the boatman. "I can catch a bite while we're moving and still lend a hand at pushing if you need one."

Poling out into the river, Blunt and Studs headed the boat upriver again. The current flowed slowly here, and several times the keel scraped bottom where the water shoaled, but each time the grating of the bottom sounded, the boatmen made the extra effort to push ahead.

Daylight was full and the sun was hitting the tops of the occasional stand of cottonwoods that stood on the rim of the ledges when the bottom of the johnboat scraped again. The craft lurched, shuddered for a moment, then came to a halt. Both boatmen leaned with extra pressure on their poles, and Longarm jumped to grab the pole he'd been using, but even when he added his efforts the boat stayed motionless, not even swaying in the gently roiling current of the brown water.

"Looks like we hit it too good," Blunt said. "But if it

hadn't've grounded here, there ain't much chance we could go on much further anyways."

"How far ahead is this place we're headed for?" Longarm asked. He looked around, but all that he could see were the ocher-earthed sides of the bluffs that rose a hundred yards away on both sides of the stream's banks.

"Oh, it's a good twelve miles by the river," Blunt told him. "Not that far on foot, though, eight or ten'd be more like it."

"Well, that ain't too bad," Longarm frowned. "A man can walk that without it hurting him much."

"I guess so," Blunt nodded. "But we might be able to get off this shoal. If all three of us gets back here in the stern and we jump and move around, we can get free and push over to the bank."

"Let's give it a try," Longarm nodded.

"Come on back here, Studs," Blunt said to his helper. "It looks like it's time to do what we figured to."

Studs began making his way to the stern. He'd reached the seat where Longarm stood when his foot slipped and he threw out his arms for balance.

"Give me a hand, Custis!" he cried.

Longarm leaned forward and extended his hands. Studs grabbed them and locked his fingers into Longarm's.

Longarm heard the scraping of Blunt's feet behind him, then something hard crashed down on his head and he knew nothing more.

Chapter 9

When consciousness first returned, Longarm was aware of only one thing: his head was throbbing as though it would never stop. He ignored the pain and tested his bonds. His wrists were bound together tightly and pulled down to his waist by a second rope just below his belt that held them to his body. Though the bonds that confined his wrists were cutting into his flesh, he felt them give an infinitesimal amount as he tried to stretch the rope by spreading his hands and flexing his wrists.

His testing took less than a minute, but even the slight movements that he could make helped to clear his head. Now he could hear the thudding of his captors' feet on the johnboat's bottom planking. Closing his eyes, he stayed motionless again. The scraping thud of boots came closer. Then Studs's voice broke the silence.

"You must've landed a real good one on him, Blunt. He's still out."

"Oh, I hit him hard. I wanted to be sure I'd put him out for a while. He's got the look of a real gunhand, and I ain't right anxious to give one of his kind a chance to draw."

"Looks like to me you might've finished him."

"Nah. He's just plumb under," Blunt said. "He won't be giving us no trouble for a while."

"Let's see how much he's got on him, then," Studs suggested. "Then we'll finish him off and hang a rock on him and shove him overboard, like we done the others."

Longarm had expected something of the kind. Now, hearing the outlaw's suggestion, he realized that he had no time to waste in getting free. From the sound of the river pirates' voices they were standing only a foot or so from his head, but he knew that opening his eyes to look might result in instant death.

"Ah, it's too crowded in the boat," Blunt objected.

Under any other circumstances, Longarm might have uttered a sigh of relief at the river pirate's words, but he realized that the two men were probably looking at him and he lay quietly.

Blunt went on, "He ain't gonna be coming around very fast. And there ain't likely to be nobody passing by here. We got plenty of time to shore the boat and see how much he's got on him. Then we'll hang a rock on his belt and push out to the middle of the river and toss him over."

"Let's do it before he comes around, then," Studs agreed. "It'll be easier to lift him out if he can't try to fight us."

"Get as far back here with me as you can," Blunt told his partner. "I'm ready to push us off soon as the bow comes off the bottom."

Another scraping of boots on the johnboat's bottom reached Longarm's ears as the boatmen shifted around. The boat began rocking, then settled down. Longarm wasn't sure exactly where the boatmen were or whether they were watching him. He kept his eyes closed and did not move.

"That damn fool Custis didn't tumble for a minute to what we was doing," Studs went on. "If he'd been around boats any, he'd've knowed all we had to do to slip off that sandbar was for all of us to get in the stern and let the bow lift itself free."

By now Longarm had deduced what must have happened after Blunt's club had knocked him out. He had a reasonably full picture of the sequence of events, and was completely aware of the situation he was in. His mental picture told him that he was lying between the midsection and the stern of the johnboat. His back was jammed against the coarse canvas that covered the heaped bulk of the cargo; his head, twisted uncomfortably, rested on the bottom of the craft.

While he waited for the treacherous boatmen to pole the johnboat to shore, Longarm went back to work on the rope that bound his wrists. He was certain enough that his captors were devoting all their attention to freeing the boat from the sandbar and gambled that they would not notice him if he risked moving around a bit.

Twisting and flexing his arms, he pushed his bound wrists lower, then cocked his elbows out and pulled his hands up his chest until the pressure of the rope became almost unbearable. Ignoring the pain, he set his teeth and twisted his sinewy forearms. The rough hempen rope bit into his flesh, but the leverage he had created was enough to slip the knot a bit more and create a tiny bit of slack in his bonds.

Them two bastards has been planning this ever since they seen you was carrying a pretty good handful of money, old son, he told himself as he worked. *And they sure done a good job of taking you in, just like you was a rube from back East. From what they said, you ain't the first one they've robbed, either. Looks like they took you for an easy mark.*

His thoughts were interrupted by the scraping of feet on the boat's bottom. Closing his eyes, he lay still again.

In a moment the boat swayed and then, though Longarm had no sense of being in motion, he could hear the soft sound of its bow cutting through the water. A few moments later the hull grated against sand and the hiss of movement stopped.

When the johnboat bobbed and swayed as the boatmen jumped to shore and their calls and noises as they tethered the vessel reached Longarm's ears, he went back to struggling against his bonds. Blunt and Studs tugged at the mooring-rope and found a place to fasten it. Longarm had managed to get a fair amount of slack in the rope that immobilized his wrists before he heard them returning. By the time the boat swayed as the two men got back aboard, Longarm had closed his eyes and let himself go limp.

"Damned if he ain't still out," Studs commented. "You real sure you didn't hit the son of a bitch hard enough to kill him?"

"I've used that billyclub on too many thick heads not to know what I was doing," Blunt answered. "Come on, let's get him on shore while he's still out."

Longarm kept all his muscles completely relaxed. His body sagged inertly when rough hands picked him up by the ankles and armpits, and he kept his muscles slack while Blunt and Studs lifted him from the boat and carried him to shore. He did not even move when they dropped him unceremoniously on the ground.

"Might as well see what he's got on him before he comes around," Blunt suggested. "I already got his Colt, but I ain't looked in his pockets yet. That was a pretty good-sized fistful of money he pulled out back at the shanty. If I recall, he taken it outa his right-hand britches pocket. We'll get his coat out of the boat after we've cleaned out what he's got on him."

Longarm felt Blunt's hand slide into his trousers pocket and collect the money he carried there, together with the coin purse in which he had his reserve expense money.

While Blunt was groping in Longarm's pocket for the loose coins Studs said, "Get that watch outa his vest pocket while you're at it. Even if it ain't a good one it'll bring us a little bit, too."

"Oh, hell, Studs!" Blunt snapped. "Whatever kind of watch he's got, it ain't likely to be worth a lot. Leave it for now and let's count the cash. I wanta find out how much quick cash we'll make off of him."

"Suit yourself," Studs told his partner.

From the tone of Studs's voice Longarm could visualize the shrug that went with the boatman's words. He gave a silent sigh of relief at Blunt's greedy impatience, for when he bent his head as far as he dared without being noticed he could see the edge of his wallet with his badge inside sticking out of his top vest pocket.

He could also feel the weight of the stubby .44 caliber derringer which was connected to his watch chain in the bottom pockets of the vest. The boatman stepped away from him and Longarm began flexing his wrists again. Now he was rewarded for the straining and scraping he had done earlier. As he worked his wrists around and back and forth, the turns of rope that bound them loosened appreciably.

A pace or two from where he lay, Longarm could hear the clink of coins as Blunt began counting the ready cash he'd scooped out of his trouser pockets. The muted clinking of the mixture of gold and silver coins lasted several moments, then the boatman said, "If he ain't got a lot more big gold pieces in this purse, we ain't gonna do too good, Studs. Counting everything, there ain't but about sixty dollars of loose change here."

"Look in the purse, then," Studs told his partner. "Stands to reason that's where he'd carry his spare cash."

In a moment Blunt said, "Well, now. This looks better. There's six double-eagles and eight or nine half-eagles here. And there's something that feels like another double-eagle in a little leather pouch."

"Take it out and see," Studs said.

"Yep," Blunt went on after a momentary pause. "Here's another twenty, bright and shiny like it just come outa the mint. And—" he stopped short.

"And what?" Studs asked.

"Gawd Almighty!" Blunt exclaimed. "It looks to me like we made a real big mistake jumping this Custis fella, Studs."

"What the hell d'you mean?" Studs demanded.

"Take a look at this double-eagle," Blunt told his partner.

There was a moment of silence. Then Studs said slowly, "It looks just like that twenty that the Deacon showed us when he passed through last month."

"It is just like that one of the Deacon's, damn it!" Blunt exclaimed angrily. "Except it's got a different number on it. This son of a bitch Custis belongs to the Deacon's outfit!"

"Well, I don't aim to get on the wrong side of the Deacon, or Rattler Reyna, either one!" Studs protested.

"Me either," Blunt agreed. "If what the Deacon told us about works out, them two's gonna have everybody that's anybody in that new gang they're putting together!"

"They've already made a pretty good start, too, from what the Deacon let us in on," Studs reminded his partner. "And this fellow Custis is bound to be with 'em, even if I never did hear his name before."

"From the way he was acting, in such a hurry to head west, I'd guess he's from someplace way further along," Blunt said. "But that don't change nothing. He's got this marked double-eagle, and it ain't likely it'd be in his pocket unless he's tied up with Reyna and the Deacon."

Hearing the boatmen's conversation had convinced Longarm by now that what George Maledon had suggested was probably true: a new outlaw gang was being formed or had already been formed. Now Longarm was reasonably sure that the new criminal outfit was so big and its members so widely scattered out through the West that they found it necessary to use the numbered double-eagles to identify themselves to one another. His thoughts were broken into when the boatmen took up their conversation.

"If the Deacon or Reyna finds out we messed with one of their men, we're likely to wind up on the bottom of the Canadian along with Custis," Studs suggested.

"You think I don't know that?" Blunt asked. "But if we let him go and he tells them what we done, we'd be gone geese anyhow as soon as they found out about it."

"How much of a chance you think there is that they'll find out?" Studs asked thoughtfully.

Longarm could have answered all the questions raised by Blunt and Studs, but he knew that whatever he said would bring things to a climax before he'd be ready to deal with them. His efforts to free his hands had still been unsuccessful, though now he could turn his wrists inside the rope that bound them. He redoubled his attempt to work more slack into the stubborn rope that made his hands and arms useless.

Blunt answered Stud's question, saying, "There ain't much

chance they'll ever find out. Nobody's seen this Custis fellow with us except them redskins where we stopped downriver, and if he's on the owlhoot trail, they ain't likely to hear about him dropping outa sight."

"I been thinking pretty much along them lines," Studs agreed. "So I say let's get rid of him right now."

"That suits me," Blunt told his partner. "You want to do it, or you want me to?"

"Hell, it don't make all that much difference."

Longarm had still been unable to get a great deal more slack in the rope that bound his wrists.

Blunt went on, "You get back on shore and pick up a big rock, one that'll keep him from floating up when he starts to swell up. While you're getting it, I'll do the job on Custis. There ain't no use I can see for us to put it off."

Studs jumped from the johnboat to shore, setting the craft to swaying. Blunt rose to his feet. He still had Longarm's Colt tucked in his belt, and freed the weapon as he reached Longarm's recumbent form.

Longarm made one final effort to free his hands. He no longer tried to hide the fact that he had recovered consciousness. Blunt gaped in surprise when he saw Longarm moving. The revolver he'd pulled from his belt sagged in his hand as his jaw dropped.

Blunt's momentary hesitation gave Longarm a few precious seconds. Without regard to the rope scraping the skin from his wrist and the back of his hand, Longarm gave a final mighty tug that freed his right hand from its bonds.

Longarm's hand was closing on the butt of his derringer while Blunt was still frozen in astonishment. Before the outlaw boatman could raise the Colt, Longarm brought up the derringer and triggered it. He fired with the accuracy that was second nature to him after so many other such deadly encounters. The slug from the derringer went home.

Blunt's jaw stayed open but his gun hand started to sag. He triggered the Colt in his dying reflex and the slug dimpled the surface of the river a foot or more from the side of the boat. Then Blunt was crumpling slowly to the bottom of the johnboat, his jaw still dropped wide as his eyes glazed.

Longarm wasted no time. His ankles were still bound, but he did not stop to untie them. Dragging himself the short distance necessary to reach Blunt's body, he grabbed his Colt from the dead outlaw's limp hand, then swiveled toward the riverbank looking for his second antagonist.

Studs was heading toward the riverbank carrying a big rock. The boulder was so heavy that he'd been forced to use both hands to hold it. He let the rock drop when the two shots shattered the still air, but in his confidence that Blunt had fired them into Longarm he held on to the boulder a few instants too long.

Longarm's second shot took Studs squarely in the heart. The boulder fell to the ground, then Studs dropped beside it, his still form sprawling in the unmistakable limpness of death.

For a few moments Longarm did not move, but stood checking the bodies of the two river pirates sprawled on the shore. When neither of them stirred, he let go the breath he'd been holding but did not move from where he was crouching.

Methodically he reloaded his Colt and replaced it in its holster. The derringer was swinging at the end of his watch chain, and he thumbed a fresh bullet out of his gunbelt to reload it before tucking it into his vest pocket again. Only then did he reach down and tug at the knot of the rope that held his ankles lashed together.

His feet began tingling as soon as he'd loosed the bonds, and he sat down on the johnboat's nearest seat. Reaching into his vest pocket, he took out one of his long thin cigars, only to find that at some time during the rough handling he'd undergone at the hands of the dead outlaws it had broken in half. He discarded it and took out another. It was intact. Longarm fished a match from his pocket and lighted the cheroot.

Only after he'd gotten his cigar drawing satisfactorily did Longarm feel that things had gotten back to normal. He looked from one of the bodies to the other and shook his head.

Them fellows was a mite too greedy, old son, his thoughts ran. *And it's lucky for you they was. If they'd've tended to getting rid of you before they begun counting up their loot, you'd be down in the mud at the bottom of the Canadian River, and they'd be setting up here crowing. Now all you got to do is get on to the closest place where you can hire a horse and start looking for them two other outlaws they was talking about. Sure as God made little green apples, as soon as you've caught up with them, you'll turn up Gunge Peyton, too.*

Longarm stood up from the breakfast table in the Fort Elliott mess hall and said to Major Bellington, "I sure do thank you, Major, and them troopers that gave me a hand. If they hadn't spotted me and come to see if I needed help, chances are I'd still be walking along the riverbank."

"Glad we could be of service, Marshal Long," the major replied. "You know you're welcome to stay here a while longer, until you get rested up."

"Why, I thank you kindly for the invitation, but I've lost too much time off this case I'm on. I've got a dead man's trail to pick up, so I aim to head for Tascosa and see if I can find out anything there."

"I can understand how you feel," the major said. "We get on some urgent missions, too. Or did until we got the Indians settled down. By the way, I've told the officer of the day to have the squad that'll be scouting along the Canadian River take care of the bodies of those outlaws and investigate the cargo on their johnboat."

"That'll be another big help," Longarm nodded. "You and your men has been right fine. Hope I can return the favor some time along the way."

"Think nothing of it, Marshal," Bellington said. "With the Comanches finally settled down, things are so quiet here now and rotation's so slow that we don't get to see new faces too often. I'm sorry we couldn't send a telegram to your chief, but the brass in Washington's pulled the telegraph lines out of most of these Western outposts, trying to save money."

"Well, Billy Vail's used to me not reporting in regular," Longarm replied. "And pretty soon I'll get to a place where there's a railroad and a telegraph wire."

After his showdown with Blunt and Studs the previous day, Longarm had decided that the best course for him to follow was to stay with the Canadian River in spite of its crooked, circuitous course and walk until he reached the nearest town.

Carrying his saddlebags and bedroll, he'd walked in the blazing Texas sun for only a little more than two hours before three cavalrymen on patrol from Fort Elliott had seen him.

They'd ridden to investigate the phenomenon of a lone man on foot crossing the open prairie and after he'd shown his badge and explained what had happened the soldiers had invited him to ride pillion to the fort. There Longarm had been greeted cordially, and for the first time since leaving Fort Smith had enjoyed the luxury of a bath, a hot supper, and a night in a genuine bed.

With a final wave to the commandant and the officers at the breakfast table, Longarm made his way to the fort's corral. A remount horse was saddled and waiting.

"I'll leave your critter at the livery stable in Mobeetie," Longarm told the hostler sergeant as he swung into the saddle. "I guess they still got one there?"

"A livery stable and the general store about all that's left of the town now," the sergeant replied. "And since the redskins have quieted down, there's not going to be much left of this old fort pretty soon."

"Well, things come and they go," Longarm told the man. "And talking about going, I better be getting on my way if I'm going to make it to Tascosa before the next blue norther comes along and slows me down again."

Swinging into the saddle, Longarm waved a final goodbye to the sergeant and toed the horse into motion. He was in familiar territory now. He lighted a fresh cigar, and trailing a trickle of blue tobacco smoke behind him reined the horse toward the west after he'd left the fort. Ahead lay a two-day ride to Tascosa.

And if you got any luck left, old son, he told himself as he moved across the summer-high prairie grass, *that's where you'll get back on the trail of that murdering bastard Gunge Peyton.*

Chapter 10

Across the Canadian River's brown roiling waters Tascosa looked the same to Longarm as it had several years earlier, when he'd first seen the little Texas Panhandle town. Under the bright morning sun, its tan-hued adobe buildings stood squat, their angular lines broken by a few new frame business buildings and dwellings. Longarm rode a mile or so farther. Then to avoid the quicksands that dotted the riverbed closer to town, he picked a spot where the stream's ripples indicated gravelled shallows and reined his horse into the water.

Once across the river, he picked up the well-beaten cattle drive trail that led to Dodge City. Turning south, he rode at the edge of the hoof-pocked trail. Half an hour later he was on the trails as it slanted through the few houses on Tascosa's outskirts and merged with Spring Street.

At close range, Tascosa showed more changes than he had been able to make out from a distance. There were new business buildings on Spring Street now, and ahead of him, at the corner of Main Street, the Howard & McMasters General Store had added a second story to what had been a squat and rambling red brick structure. Longarm reined in at the hitchrail in front of the store, tossed the reins of the livery horse he'd rented at Mobeetie over the rail, and went inside.

"I reckon you can tell me where I'd be likely to find Jim McMasters," he said to the clerk who came up to wait on him. "This place has changed some since I stopped here last, and I don't know my way around in here any more."

"Mr. McMasters moved his office upstairs when he added the second story," the clerk replied. "The stairs are over there by the wall."

As had been the case on Longarm's first encounter with the merchant, James McMaster's office door stood open, a tacit invitation for anybody wanting to see him. When Longarm's boot heels grated on the floor, McMasters looked up from his big rolltop desk at the back wall and stood up.

"Longarm!" he exclaimed. "It's been a while since you dropped in on me. I'm real glad to see you!"

"Well, I ain't had a case bring me down this way for quite a spell," Longarm replied as the two men shook hands. "But it looks like I got some business here now."

"Sit down and tell me about it," McMasters invited. "I'd offer you a cigar, but I know you prefer those long strings you call cigars and, besides, I've given up smoking."

"I guess I got so many bad habits that one more ain't going to make much never-mind," Longarm said to the storekeeper after he had his cigar drawing well. "And I see you've changed things around a mite since I was here the last time."

"Yes, and I'm not sure it was a wise move," McMasters said soberly. "For a while it looked like we were going to get a railroad line through town, so a lot of us got excited and started building against the time when Tascosa would grow. Then the railroad brass changed their minds. I don't know why, but they built the line through a little place south of here, called Ragtown."

"So you don't stand to get the new business you figured you was going to." Longarm nodded.

"That's about the size of it," McMasters agreed. "What we

did get was a lot of undesirables who moved here for the same reason we overbuilt."

"That's what brought me here," Longarm told his old friend. "From what I've come up with in this case I'm on now, I got a hunch one of them undesirables you're talking about is either in town or he's got a hideout close to here."

"Would you care to put a name to him?"

"I'll do better'n that, Jim. I'll give you three names and see if you've heard one of 'em lately. Course, the names I know these scoundrels by might not be the ones they're travelling under now, but so far they're all I got to work on."

"Trot 'em out," McMasters invited Longarm. "If I know anything about any of them, I'll pass it on to you."

"Well, I guess we better start with Gunge Peyton."

McMasters shook his head. "Never heard of him."

"How about Rattler Reyna?"

"That's a little closer to home," the merchant nodded. "I had some trouble with a man named Reyna who used to work on the LIT. Is that the one you mean?"

"Did folks call him Rattler?"

"Either Rattler or Rattlesnake," McMasters frowned. "It's been a while since I've heard anything about him, and I can't remember exactly what his nickname was. I do recall that he was a mean one, but I don't think he stayed on after that English syndicate bought George's spread."

"From what you said, I'd guess he's the one I'm after," Longarm told McMasters. "Now I'll trot out another one. Does the name Jim Houlihan bring anybody to mind?"

McMasters shook his head. "The only Houlihan who was ever around here was an old Irishman who used to be a sailor, and he's been dead a long time."

"Well, that's the end of my list," Longarm went on. "But as long as I'm in town, I aim to drop in on Mickey McCormick. I guess he's still here?"

"I hate to tell you, Longarm, because I recall that you and him got to be pretty good friends, but Mickey's dead. He got the lung fever and just faded out overnight."

"Now, I'm real sorry to hear that," Longarm said. "And I imagine Frenchy's moved someplace else after he died?"

"No, indeed," McMasters replied. "She's still living in the house Mickey fixed up for her. There's more to it than that, though. She goes out to Mickey's grave once a week and puts flowers on it. Swears she'll keep on doing that as long as she lives."

Longarm frowned thoughtfully. "You know, when Frenchy was working down in the red light district here and in Mobeetie, she got pretty well acquainted with a lot of shady characters. She helped me on that case I had here before, and I was figuring on talking to Mickey and her to see if I can find something out from her."

"She might not talk to you," McMasters warned. "She's shut herself up in that house Mickey built for her, and doesn't go anywhere except the cemetery. She won't let anybody in to visit her, won't even come downtown to buy groceries. When she needs something from the store, she sends one of 'Sidro Serna's kids to buy it for her."

"Well, all I can do is try," Longarm told the storekeeper. "I'll go on over to her house and see what I can do. Then I'll duck in here an bid you goodbye before I ride out again."

Walking down Main Street from the store, Longarm turned up Bridge Street for a block. The small neat cottage Mickey McCormick had built for his bride stood on the corner of Bridge and Court Street. Looking at it, Longarm could see no sign that the house was occupied. The blinds were closed on the windows along its side, but only inside roll-up shades covered the windows at the front.

Mounting the steps, Longarm knocked. He waited for several moments and knocked again. Out of the corner of his eye, he saw a slight movement in one of the shades at a window beside the door. In a moment the door swung open and Frenchy McCormick appeared.

"Longarm," she said. "You're the last person I expected to see here, and there's not many besides you that I'd open this door for."

"Now, that's as nice a compliment as any I ever got," Longarm told her.

"I guess you're here because you've heard about..."

Frenchy hesitated for a moment and went on, "About Mickey dying so suddenly."

"I just heard about him from Jim McMasters," Longarm said. "And I'm real sorry, Frenchy. I'd have come to tell you that, even if I didn't have any business with you."

"Business?" Frenchy McCormick frowned. "What kind of business could you possibly have with me?"

"Well, it ain't all that big of a thing, but I'd feel a lot easier if you was to ask me to step inside where we can talk private," he suggested.

Again Frenchy hesitated. Then she nodded and moved out of the doorway. Longarm stepped past her into the living room of the cottage. Frenchy closed the door and indicated a chair. Longarm sat down and she took a chair close to him.

Looking at her, Longarm again decided that he'd been right in thinking what he had the first time he'd seen her, that Frenchy McCormick was a beautiful woman. Though her face now showed lines of grief at the corners of her eyes and mouth, her high forehead was still smooth and unlined, and the shining black hair that fell in smooth ripples down her back and the small curls above her ears contained no strands of gray.

She was wearing a black sateen dress that did not conceal the swells of her breasts as she sat straight in her chair, her shoulders squared. It was as hard this time as it had been when Longarm first met her for him to realize that she'd spent most of her early life as a prostitute, first in Mobeetie, then in Tascosa, where she'd met and married Mickey.

Frenchy sat silently for a moment, and when Longarm did not begin talking at once she finally opened their conversation.

"If you've been in town very long, I suppose you've heard a lot of stories about how I've gone crazy since Mickey died," she said. "And about how I shut myself up here all the time."

"I had a talk with Jim McMasters," Longarm told her. "He said you been sorta keeping off to yourself."

"That's what I want to do," Frenchy confessed. "When Mickey died I guess I realized that nobody lives forever. All I

97

want is to be by myself, here in this house, and remember the good days we had in it together."

"Well, I ain't going to lie to you and say I know how you feel, because I don't," Longarm told her. "But if that's what you want to do, I sure wouldn't make no remarks about it or try to get you to change. Matter of fact, the business I said I had is to ask you about the name of a man you might've run across before you and Mickey met up."

Smiling faintly, Frenchy said, "I did meet a lot of men, Longarm. But none after I fell in love with Mickey."

"This one might've struck in your mind, though," Longarm went on. "Rattler Reyna. Jim McMasters said he knew a fellow named Reyna that used to be a hand on the LIT."

Frenchy was silent for a moment, then she nodded slowly and said, "Now that you've brought the name up, I do remember a ranch hand whose friends called him Rattler. But that was a long time ago, Longarm. I doubt that he's anywhere in this part of the country now."

"You got any idea where he came from?"

Frenchy shook her head. "No. But it seems to me that somebody made a remark after I'd moved here about the Rattler leaving and going to Dodge."

"Dodge City? Up in Kansas?"

"Yes. Not the one up in Iowa or wherever it is."

"But you ain't heard about him lately, though?"

"Not for several years. I think the only reason I remember him at all is because of the way he talked."

"You mean he talked like most Mexicans, or different?"

"Different. He had a great big gap between the two top front teeth, and he sort of hissed. I guess that's one reason his friends called him Rattler. That, and because he was so mean."

"Well, he ought not to be too hard to run down, then."

"Not that it matters to me, Longarm" Frenchy said. "But is he in trouble with the law?"

"He might be. I ain't sure yet. I'll know more after I get to wherever he hangs out these days."

"That means you'll be moving on, then?"

"Soon as I make sure nobody's seen this Reyna fellow

around town lately," Longarm replied. He stood up. "Well, Frenchy, I do thank you for helping me again. Now, you take good care of yourself and try to stop all this grieving. It ain't going to bring your man back to you."

"I know that, Longarm," she replied. "But Mickey was the best man I ever knew. It's going to take me the rest of my life to forget him, and I'm not sure that I even want to."

"Make a try," Longarm said. "And it's a pretty sure bet I'll get a case sooner or later that'll bring me back to Tascosa. When I do, I'll stop by again and see how you're getting on."

When the conductor came through the cars calling the Dodge City stop, Longarm was leaning back against the green plush of his seat in the smoker, puffing on a cigar. During the trip he'd almost caught up on the sleep he'd lost while riding from Tascosa to Ragtown in order to make his train connections, and the long roundabout ride to Dodge City had given him time to think about his case.

You still ain't a lot further ahead than you was when you started out from Denver, old son, he mused. *Seems like every time you get a little ways along on a hot trail it just sorta peters out and you got to go back and start all over again. But someplace up ahead, there's going to be a place where this damn trail quits zigzagging and ends.*

In a few moments the coach couplings began banging as the engineer applied the brakes. The train came to a slow stop. Longarm picked up his gear and made his way to the door.

Walking toward the center of town, his rifle in his left hand balancing his saddlebags in his right, Longarm saw that Dodge City had changed very little since his last visit. The signs on the high-rising false fronts over the swinging doors of the three biggest and most popular saloons—the Lady Gay, the Long Branch, and the Saratoga—still dominated the section of Front Street popularly called "the Plaza."

Loungers still loafed in front of any of the buildings which had a shaded facade or provided an entryway wide enough to have room on its steps for a man with nothing else to do. On the opposite side of the dusty wagonwheel-rutted street the office of the city marshal drew its accustomed share of loafers. Longarm angled across the street, picked his way through the loafers, and went inside. A stranger sat in the chair at the town marshal's desk.

"You're in charge here, I suppose?" Longarm asked.

"Sure looks that way, don't it?" the man at the desk drawled, inspecting Longarm's wrinkled, travel-stained clothes and the stubble of beard that had sprouted on his jaws during the two-day train journey. "You looking for anybody special to be?"

Longarm shook his head. Though the city marshal's insolent manner irritated him, he kept his face expressionless and his voice level as he replied.

"No. I just wondered. The way they got here in Dodge of shooting city marshals before they can get their badges pinned on, a man never knows who he's gonna find holding down the job if he ain't paid a visit here for a week or more." While he talked, Longarm had slipped his wallet out of his pocket. He flipped it open to show his own badge. "Name's Custis Long. Deputy U. S. Marshal outa Denver."

"Well, I'll be damned!" the local man said as he studied the badge. "You'd be the one they call Longarm, I bet!"

"I answer to it about as quick as I do my right name."

"I've sure heard a lot about you," the Dodge officer went on. "But the town's been cleaned up a lot, and I aim to keep it that way. My name's Tom Nixon, by the way, Marshal Long."

"Glad to meet you," Longarm replied as he shook Nixon's outstretched hand.

"I don't guess this is just a friendly visit?" Nixon asked.

Longarm shook his head. "Not hardly. I'm trying to run down two men, but I'll ask you about another one first. Was there another deputy U. S. marshal here asking questions a little while back? His name was Jim Houlihan."

Nixon shook his head. "No. And I'd know if he had been."

"Likely you would," Longarm agreed. "But I was pretty sure he didn't get this far. Now, one of the others is a killer named Gunge Peyton. You ever hear his name mentioned around here?"

Nixon shook his head. "Not that I recall. And that's a name I wouldn't forget, if he's travelling under it."

"Which ain't likely," Longarm nodded. "I ain't got a clue that'd tie him in here at Dodge anyhow. The other one's a Mexican fellow they call Rattler Reyna, or maybe Rattlesnake Reyna. The last I heard of him, he'd headed this way from Tascosa."

"If he ever got here, I sure haven't run into him, or even heard about him," Nixon frowned. "But like you guessed, I haven't been in Dodge all that long."

"Who's left around here that might know?"

"Well, let's see," Nixon frowned thoughtfully. "I'd guess the best place you can start is across the street. Go over to the Lady Gay and talk to Al Updegraf."

"You mean he's still alive?" Longarm asked. "I heard Bat Masterson had gunned him down a while back."

"Bat winged him, all right," Nixon nodded. "But it wasn't up to his regular grade of shooting. He just put a bullet in Al's shoulder. Al got over it without any trouble, and he's back on the job over at the Lady Gay now."

"If you don't mind me leaving my stuff here for a little while, I'll step across the street and have a talk with Al. I guess Bat Masterson shook the town's dust off his heels after the shooting?" While he talked, Longarm put his saddlebags and rifle in the corner behind Nixon's desk and tossed his blanket roll on top of them.

"He made himself scarce," Nixon replied. "From what I've heard, he's gone back to Tombstone again."

"I'll palaver with Al for a minute, then," Longarm said. "I guess he is about the likeliest fellow close around that might give me a lead on that Reyna rascal."

Crossing the street again, Longarm pushed through the bat-wings of the Lady Gay Saloon. He didn't recognize the man behind the bar watching him in the mirror until he'd gotten close enough to raise his foot to the rail. Then, as the barkeep turned around, he saw that it was the man he was seeking.

"How're you holding up, Al?" he asked.

Updegraf was turning toward him as he spoke and at the

same time extended his hand. As he and Longarm shook, he said, "I guess I'm doing about as good as I got a right to expect. You heard about me and Bat Masterson tangling up?"

"Just a minute ago, when that young fellow you got acting sorta like he's the town marshal told me you was here."

"Well, stand right where you are for a minute," the saloon man went on. "I got what's left of that bottle of Tom Moore Rye you had me order special for you tucked away, and unless you've changed a lot, you'll be asking for it next."

"I sure ain't changed all that much, Al," Longarm said. "And I reckon I'm due a drink after that long train ride I had."

While Longarm was talking the bar owner had been rummaging below the bar. He came up with the bottle of Tom Moore and poured Longarm a generous tot. Longarm took a healthy swallow and put the half-empty glass on the bar, and Updegraf filled it to the brim again.

"What brings you here to Dodge?" he asked while he was pouring. "It's been a while since I seen you."

"I'm working a case, like always," Longarm replied. "And that's got me looking for two men. One's a killer named Gunge Peyton. The other one's been around Dodge a while, his name's Reyna. I hope you know whether he's still around here or not."

"He'd be the one they call Rattler?" Updegraf asked. "A mean son of a bitch?"

"I never have run across him before, but that sounds about right, from what I've heard."

"Sure, he was here a while," the saloon-keeper nodded. "Him and the Masterson bunch never did hit it off too good, though, so Rattler Reyna taken off. He'd gone to Colorado the last I heard, someplace down in the southwest part of the Uncompahgre foothill country."

Longarm was sipping the Tom Moore while Updegraf talked. He swallowed the rest of the rye after the saloon man gave him the clue he'd been seeking, then said, "Well, I'm much obliged to you, Al. You've told me what I was after. And that's a big help."

"Then what're you looking so sour about?" Updegraf asked.

"Because I ain't had time to sit still since I left Denver on this case," Longarm replied. "It ain't been a half-hour since I stepped off the train, and what you just told me means I got to go take another long train ride."

Chapter 11

Longarm was only half-awake when the train that had been rattling his bones since he'd boarded it at Dodge City pulled to a stop at the depot in Walsenberg. The weariness that came from almost a month of constant travel and little sleep was overtaking even his sturdy muscles.

A quarter of an hour earlier, when the conductor passed through the smoking car calling the Walsenberg station stop, Longarm had been half-tempted to stay on the train as it went on to Denver, where he'd be sure of getting a full night of undisturbed sleep and a change of clothes. The thought had been a fleeting one, and he'd abandoned it as soon as it occurred.

You've got this far, old son, he told himself. *And even if it's sorta like trying to find a needle in a haystack, you got a pretty fair lead to run down. So the only thing to do is keep on pushing. Maybe Billy'll put you on that courtroom duty you missed when this case come along, and that'll give you all the time you need to catch up on the sleep you lost.*

Standing up and stretching, Longarm got his gear together and walked up the aisle to the coach door. Except for one man standing beside a heap of luggage, the station platform was deserted.

"Excuse me, stranger," the man said as Longarm passed. "I have to change trains here, and I wonder if you can tell me how to get to the other depot."

"Well, it ain't all that far," Longarm replied. "But you got a load there that'll match the one I'm toting. I'd say the best thing for you to do is hire a hack, like I'm aiming to."

Longarm was taking stock of the man as he spoke. The worried-looking passenger was probably in his late thirties or early forties. He was a broad-faced, stocky man of middle height, the squareness of his untanned, clean-shaven face with its broad stubbed nose reflected in his broad-chested, wide-hipped body. He had cold gray eyes, with thin brows and stubby lashes. His hands were not those of a man who did a great deal of labor.

He had on a checked suit, its black-and-white pattern just a bit too conservative to be classed as a gambler's attire. A pearl-gray derby was on his head and his white collar showed that it had been fresh before he got on the train; now it was smutted with coal dust. Longarm glanced at the stranger's waist, looking for a gunbelt, but he wore none, and there was no telltale bulge of a pistol showing in the lines of his coat.

"I've already tried that," the man said, shaking his head. "I looked around outside, but there weren't any."

"That's on account of the railroad tracks are between the town and the station," Longarm told him. "And the street to the depot don't go across 'em. I don't guess anybody told you that, did they?"

"No. But I got off without waiting for the conductor. I guess if I'd waited, he'd have said something."

"Likely would've," Longarm agreed. "Well, if you'll pick up your bags and come along, I'll show you where you got to go. It ain't but a step, and I'm going that way myself."

Shaking his head, the stranger picked up his suitcases and followed Longarm out of the depot, across a strip of ankle-turning gravel and two sets of rails, to a dead-end street where a ramshackle hackney cab stood, the driver slouched in the seat.

When he saw Longarm and the stranger approaching he sat up straight and called, "Here you are, gents! If you're going to the Denver & Rio Grande depot, you ain't got time to do no lallygagging around. If you'll step lively and get in my cab, now, I'll get you there in plenty of time to catch your train."

"Since there's not another hack around, it looks like we'll have to share this one," the stranger told Longarm. "I hope you don't mind."

"Not a bit. Let's toss our gear in and get started," Longarm suggested.

He waited until the man had pushed his bags into the cab, piled his own belongings on top of the man's suitcases, gestured for the stranger to climb in, and followed him. Almost before Longarm's feet were in the cab, the hackman slapped the reins over his horse's rump. Longarm tried to keep his balance, but toppled back into the seat, barely missing being dumped on top of the man who'd gotten in first.

Turning to his fellow passenger, he said, "Sorry, friend. I hope I didn't step on your toes or nothing like that."

"No harm done at all," the other nodded. "I'm just glad that we both got in."

"One thing sure, I'd hate to miss making connections and have to spend the night here," Longarm said. "And the D&RG ain't going to hold up that train we got to catch, seeing as they don't even know we're coming."

"This town doesn't look like it'd be much of a place to spend the night in," his fellow passenger remarked as the cab entered Walsenberg's main street. It was deserted, the stores dark, the street empty. Only the lights around the batwings of two or three saloons broke the darkness.

"Well, Walsenberg ain't much more'n a whistle stop," Longarm said. "And was I you, I wouldn't look for much on that train we're going to be getting on, either."

"You talk like you've ridden it before."

"More'n once. It ain't nothing but an accommodation train for the silver mines up in the Uncompahgres, around Del

107

Norte and Creede. It just runs up as far as Silverton with empty ore cars and picks up full ones to bring back here to the smelter."

"But it does carry passengers, I've been told," the other man frowned.

"Oh, sure. It's got one passenger coach, but that's all."

"One seat in that passenger car's all I'm interested in," the man smiled. "So I'm not worrying too much. When I get to Silverton, there'll be a guide waiting to show me the rest of the way."

"You're a stranger here, I take it?"

"Around this part of Colorado, I am, even if it's not too far from home. I'm from Albuquerque."

"Well, I call Denver home myself," Longarm said. "But I ain't been up in the Uncompahgre country for quite a spell."

"And I've never been there before. By the way, my name's Anders," the man said.

"Mine's Long," Longarm said, extending his hand.

After their handshake, Anders gestured toward Longarm's saddlebags and bedroll, piled on the seat across from them, and said casually, "With all that gear, it looks to me like you're planning to go past the end of the railroad line, which is what I happen to be doing myself."

"Oh, I got some travelling to do beyond Silverton," Longarm replied noncommittally. "But it ain't the first time."

By now the hack had reached the end of the street, and as the cabman guided his horse through its abrupt and surprising turns they could see a glow of light ahead. When they'd gone a bit farther they could see that the light was spilling out of the D&RG depot's open freight door. Its glow picked up the passenger coach that stood on the tracks beside the station.

"It looks to me like we're getting to the depot," Anders commented. "So we ought to make our train."

"Sure does," Longarm answered as the hack veered to one side again. "It ain't pulled out yet, but from the steam it's making it ain't going to be long before it does. This hack's going to have to move a lot faster."

Even before they'd covered half the distance to the D&RG depot, they saw they would be too late. The whistle of the

engine sounded the twin toots which signalled the train's de-
parture and the back-end lanterns of the coach began to move.

Opening the hack's door, Longarm leaned out and called
up to the cabbie, "Ain't there a place up ahead where you can
catch up with that train?"

"None I know of," the hackman replied. He'd begun rein-
ing in when he saw the train pulling out. "There ain't no
streets or roads on past the depot. No, sir," he went on as he
turned the horse and started back toward Walsenberg. "Looks
like you'll have to stay over here till the next train leaves."

"When's that?" Longarm asked.

"Why, this time tomorrow," the hackie said. "That ain't a
regular-run passenger train, you know. It's as apt to leave a
mite early as it is to run late. All it hauls is ore-carts from the
mines down to the smelter here, then takes the empties back
up. That passenger coach is just an accommodation."

"I guess our luck's run out," Longarm told Anders as he
swung back into the cab and settled into his seat.

"So I heard. I suppose we don't have any choice but to
spend the night here and take tomorrow's train."

"Not unless we get some horses. And even if we done that,
the train tomorrow night'd still get us there quicker."

"I suppose you're right," Anders nodded. "But the delay
won't matter a great deal to me. How about you?"

"Oh, I can stand it," Longarm said.

"I suppose there's a hotel here?"

"There wasn't none last time I passed through," Longarm
replied. "But there's two or three rooming houses, as I recall.
We'll be able to find a bed someplace. If we don't, I can get a
little ways outside town and spread my bedroll."

They'd gotten close enough to the center of town now to
see the lights of the first saloon. Anders gestured toward it and
said, "I'd like a drink before we turn in. Maybe you feel the
same way? At least it'd take the edge off our bad luck."

"A tot'd go down real good," Longarm agreed. He leaned
out of the hack's window and called to the cabbie, "I guess
you'd know some place in town where we can get a bed for
tonight? And which one of the saloons is the best?"

"Sure," the man answered. "I'll take you to Miz Leila Bissel's rooming house. It's right up ahead. She runs a nice clean place, and the best saloon in town's just a step away on Main Street. It's the Stockman's Saloon. They run honest games and don't cut the liquor and if you're hungry, that saloon's got the only free lunch in town."

"Go on to the rooming house, then," Longarm told the hackie. He turned to Anders and said, "I reckon you heard what he told me. I figured you wouldn't mind if I said yes for both of us."

"I don't mind a bit," Anders replied. "As a matter of fact, except that the man who's meeting me in Silverton might be wondering why I didn't make the train, I won't mind spending a little time in that saloon he mentioned. It'll give me a chance to see if I'm missing any bets in mine."

"You're a saloonkeeper, then, in Albuquerque?"

"I bought my place there a few years ago," Anders nodded. "It's in the new part of town, just down the main street from the Harvey House and the Santa Fe depot. I call it the First Chance, because the Harvey House is temperance and the Santa Fe cuts off its diner in Trinidad and picks up another one out of Albuquerque."

"I don't reckon I know your place," Longarm said. "But I ain't been in Albuquerque for quite a spell."

"Well, you'll be welcome anytime you're in the neighborhood."

"Thanks. I'll keep it in mind."

As Longarm spoke, the hackman reined off Main Street and pulled up his horse in front of a large white two-story house. Its windows were all dark, but a hall light was shining through the etched glass panel of the front door.

Longarm said, "I'll toss my gear out so's you can get to yours. From what the hackie said, we ain't likely to be turned away from here, but from the looks of the place the landlady's gone to bed, so I don't guess we'll need to hurry."

Carrying his rifle, he got out and pulled his bedroll and saddlebags off Anders's suitcases. He left them beside the hack, strode up the bricked walkway leading to the porch, and pulled at the doorbell. He could hear it tinkle faintly somewhere in the house, and when there was no immediate re-

110

sponse he turned back and walked to the hack. Anders had unloaded his luggage and was handing the cabman some money.

"I'll pay my share of the fare," Longarm said.

"Nonsense," Anders told him. "I owe you more than a little bit of loose change for the help you gave me."

"You owe me nothing," Longarm replied, "but I'll buy the drinks when we get over to the saloon."

"We'll settle that later," Anders replied, then nodded toward the house. "It looks like somebody's coming to the door."

Longarm turned and saw a suggestion of movement in the dimly lighted hall. He and Anders started toward the house, and just as they reached it the door opened.

A statuesquely tall woman stood in the doorway. Her long blond hair was swept back from her high forehead and cascaded down her back. Her face was full, her eyes a deep blue, and she blinked them as though to clear away her drowsiness as she looked at the two men.

"You'd be Miz Bissel, I guess?" Longarm asked.

"Yes, I'm Leila Bissel," she replied.

Anders picked up the conversation. "We just missed our train and need a place to stay tonight. The hackman said you might have a vacant room."

"I usually do," she replied. "And I do tonight. If you want to share a room, it'll be a dollar apiece. If you want singles, it's a dollar and a half. In advance."

"If it's all the same to you, I guess we better have a room apiece," Longarm told her.

He turned to Anders as he spoke and the saloonkeeper nodded in silent confirmation. Both he and Anders dug into their pockets and handed Mrs. Bissel the rent.

"I guess you'll be settling in then," she said. "I'll get you a towel apiece and fill the pitchers in your rooms. If you need more than a pitcherful, the well's out back, right outside the hall door. So is the outhouse. The rooms are right down the hall here, number four and number five."

"We're going over to the saloon for a nightcap," Anders

111

said. "Suppose we just leave our luggage in the hall and settle in later?"

"I never argue with my guests," Mrs. Bissel replied. She reached for a rack of keys on the wall behind her and selected three. Handing them to Longarm, she went on, "One's for the front door, the others are for the rooms. I'll leave you men to decide which room you take. They're both just about alike."

"We'll work that out when we come back," Longarm nodded. "Right now, both of us is more interested in getting a drink and maybe a bite to eat."

"Just be sure you lock the front door after you when you leave and come back, that's all I ask," she said. "Now, if you don't need anything more, I'll fix your rooms and get back to bed."

Longarm and Anders walked across the deserted street and pushed through the batwings of the Stockman's Saloon. Only a handful of men were in the saloon. There were three or four along the bar, laughing and talking, and the barkeep stood idle at the far end.

Except for a postage-stamp-sized dance area, the remainder of the spacious room was filled with octagonal gaming tables, though only two were in use. A game of five-hand euchre was being played at one, and four men were playing poker at another. The remaining tables were deserted; so were the chuck-a-luck table and the faro layout.

"Looks like a dull night," Anders commented. "I'd go broke if I didn't get more customers than this."

"Well, this town ain't as big as Albuquerque," Longarm said. "I guess it fills up some on Saturdays when the hands come in from the ranches."

"I suppose so," Anders nodded. "Only I'd be broke in a hurry if I had to depend on this kind of trade. But that's not here or there. Let's go over to the bar and have our drink."

Seeing Longarm and Anders approaching the bar roused the barkeep to movement. He walked up to them and nodded.

"What's your pleasure, gents?" he asked.

"I'll have a tot of Tom Moore, if you got any," Longarm told the barman. "If you ain't, I'll settle for some other good Maryland rye."

"Make mine Kentucky sour mash. Green Valley'll do fine," Anders said. "And I see a bottle of it right behind you there on your backbar."

"I'll have to step down to the other end for your rye," the barkeep said to Longarm. He reached for the bourbon bottle and set it in front of Anders, together with a shot-glass, and started toward the rear of the bar.

"These are on me," Anders told Longarm, reaching into his trousers pocket. "You've been right helpful, Mr. Long, and—" He broke off and pulled his hand out of his pocket, then went on as he freed the bottom button of his shirt and slipped his hand into the gap. Seeing Longarm's puzzled look, he went on, "When I travel, all I carry in my pockets is tip money. The rest is in my money belt, just in case I get careless, or somebody holds up the train I'm on."

"Well, I'd say that's a pretty good idea," Longarm nodded. "If everybody was as careful as you, there might not be as many holdups as there is nowadays."

Anders had pulled a long leather coin purse from the gap in his shirt. He thumbed the snap open and upended the purse into the palm of his hand. A small cascade of gold coins poured from its mouth. There were eagles, double-eagles, and half-eagles in the assortment of coins.

There was also a square leather packet Longarm recognized immediately. It was a twin to the one he had found on Jim Houlihan's body, and which he now carried tucked away in his own wallet.

Chapter 12

For a moment Longarm was tempted to arrest Anders instantly and get him safely handcuffed before asking him any questions. Then, though he still had no doubt that the leather packet in his companion's hands was identical with the one in his own pocket, second thoughts came quickly.

Old son, he told himself while he watched Anders's stubby fingers picking out coins from the gold pieces in his cupped palm, *you sure was playing in luck when you didn't tell this Anders which side of the law you're on. Now, you got to figure out which way Anders is apt to jump before you yell frog. If you can cotton up to him proper, he'll likely lead you right to the place you're looking for.*

Anders wouldn't be in these parts unless he's on his way to the hideout that new gang's got in the Uncompahgres. And that's the answer to why Jim Houlihan got killed where you found him. Gunge Peyton had to lay low. He wasn't going to risk taking no train, so he figured to circle around where there ain't so many towns, and go up from the south. Now, you got a real good chance to get this Anders to lead you to that hideout. All you need to do is play your cards smooth and easy.

Longarm's plan formed in his mind almost instantly. Looking around at the empty tables, he waited until the barkeep came back with the bottle of Tom Moore, then picked up the whiskey and the glass the barkeep had put beside it.

"I don't know about you," he said to Anders, "but I like to set down and be comfortable when I take a drink. Why don't we just take our liquor over to one of the empty tables and give our feet a rest?"

"I hadn't thought about it, but if you're more comfortable sitting, I don't see any reason to stand up."

Carrying their bottles and glasses, Longarm and Anders moved toward the tables. Longarm insinuated himself into the lead as they went through the gaming area and stopped at a table far enough removed from those around it to be private. They settled down.

Longarm lighted a fresh cigar before filling his glass and sipping the smooth but sharp-edged rye. Then he turned to Anders and said, "I ain't aiming to be nosy, but when you emptied out your purse back there at the bar I couldn't help seeing something you got in it that looked mighty interesting."

"Money's always interesting to me, too," Anders smiled.

"Oh, I wasn't talking about the money," Longarm said quickly. He reached into his pocket and took out his own purse. Instead of dumping its contents into his hand as the other man had done, he fingered the coins until he found the leather packet. Bringing it out, he laid it on the table between them.

Anders's eyebrows lifted in surprise, but this was the only change in his impassive face. He stared across the table at Longarm for a moment, then unbuttoned his shirt again, took out his own purse, and extracted the leather packet. Holding it up for Longarm to see, he said, "It appears we're heading for the same place."

"It sure looks that way," Longarm nodded.

Before he could say anything more, Anders's arm moved

with the smooth speed of a professional gambler. He dropped his own packet on the table and picked up Longarm's as he said, "You know what we're supposed to do?"

"Sure," he nodded. His expression did not change any more than his companion's had, and he made no move to do anything.

When they'd moved to the table, habit had led Longarm to take a seat facing the saloon's swinging door. His eyes went to the batwings when they swung open, and he recognized a familiar face. The man coming into the saloon was one Longarm knew very well. He was Ed Graves, a former police sergeant in Denver, and as he passed through the swinging doors Longarm also saw that Graves still wore the star badge of a lawman on his shirt.

Longarm started to drop his head, hoping that the broad brim of his new Stetson would hide his face, but Graves had already seen and recognized him. His face crinkling into a smile, he started across the floor toward the table where Longarm and Anders were sitting.

"Longarm!" Graves exclaimed loudly. "You're about the last man I'd have expected to see in Walsenberg! What kind of a case has brought you down here from Denver? Why haven't you stopped in at the city hall to say hello to me?"

An instant after Graves had called out his name, Longarm saw Anders's hand start moving. He knew that there was only one reason: to draw a gun that had escaped the close scrutiny he'd given the saloonkeeper.

Longarm's razor-honed actions showed the result of many close encounters before this one. He pushed hard on the floor with his boot heels and tilted his chair backward. At the same time, his hand found the butt of his Colt in its cross-draw holster. As his chair began leaning he swept the revolver out and fired. He was still in the chair, toppling to the floor, when Anders's dying reflex triggered the Baby LeMat he'd drawn from a belly holster that had been hidden under the bulge of his belt buckle.

Though the impact of the heavy slug from Longarm's Colt sent Anders skewing aside from the table in his chair, his dying spasm had tightened his trigger finger to fire not only

117

the single slug from the Baby LeMat's upper barrel, but the shotgun shell that was in the truncated barrel below.

Lead pellets beat a tattoo on the tabletop and smashed the bottles and glasses on it. Though he'd been sure of his shooting in the instant he'd triggered his Colt, Longarm pushed himself away from the table and toppled backward in his chair.

When the slugs from the shotgun shell began thunking and scraping and breaking the bottles and glasses as they ricocheted across the top of the sturdy table, Longarm had fallen far enough for them to pass over him harmlessly—all except one shotgun pellet, which twitched at the crown of his new Stetson and lifted it from his head.

Landing on the floor with a thud, Longarm kicked the chair out of his way and rolled to one side, then lifted himself to his knees, the Colt in his hand poised and ready. A glance at Anders, crumpled now in the skewed chair, told him no second shot would be needed. The dead man's body was still sliding slowly to the floor, his head falling forward, his arms dangling limp, the Baby LeMat in his right hand slipping out of his lifeless fingers.

Across the room, Ed Graves stood agape, his hand still on the butt of the holstered revolver he'd started to draw when his call to Longarm had triggered the gunplay. The few gamblers at the tables had not yet gotten to their feet; they were sitting in their chairs gazing through the gunsmoke.

Graves was the first to break the silence. Looking at Longarm, his face drawn into a troubled frown, he asked, "What in hell happened to start the shooting?"

"I hate to tell you, Ed," Longarm replied, "but I reckon it was you showing up and yelling my name that done it."

"Well, how was I to know?" Graves demanded, starting toward Longarm.

"Oh, I ain't blaming you," Longarm told him. He kept his voice level and spoke mildly, even though he knew Anders's death would mean that his half-formed plan to find the outlaw gang's hideout would now have to be scrapped. "You didn't have no way of knowing, any more'n I knew you'd come pushing in here."

"I'm sorry I messed things up for you, Longarm," Graves apologized. "Is there anything I can do to help?"

"You might sorta take hold of things here," Longarm said as he holstered his revolver. "Go over to whichever of them fellows by the bar owns this place, tell him I'm a lawman and shot that outlaw when he started to draw on me. While you're doing that, I'll go through the dead man's pockets. Then, if you'll take care of having the undertaker haul him away to bury, I'll be right obliged to you."

With Graves taking care of the small group of men in the saloon and keeping them from crowding up, Longarm searched Anders's body. His pockets yielded nothing except a handkerchief and pocketknife and a ticket on the Denver & Rio Grande for passage from Walsenberg to the end of the track at Creede.

In the dead man's purse, which still lay open on the table, there was what Longarm's quick glance told him was several hundred dollars in gold and silver coins, as well as a thick sheaf of paper money. The leather packet Anders had so deftly switched for Longarm's was still on the table. So was the packet Longarm had found on Jim Houlihan's body. Both square cases were soaked with spilled liquor and were slick and hard to handle when Longarm picked them up.

Longarm had not yet seen the coin in Andes's packet. He opened it now and slid the gold piece out. As he'd expected, it was a double-eagle, like the one he'd taken from Houlihan's body. He turned it and inspected the reverse side. The tiny engraved copperhead snake was in the triangle formed by the eagle's outspread wings and across from it, in the matching triangle, there was the figure 39 in miscroscopically fine lines.

You sure wasn't wrong when you made your guess, he told himself silently as he restored the coin to its case. *That Anders fellow was one of the new gang, and it's growing right fast if that gold piece you got outa Jim Houlihan's boot was only number three and this one's thirty-nine. If you hadn't put a bullet through him, you might've found out a lot more'n you know about that bunch of crooks he was tied in with. But what's done can't be undone, and what ain't been done's still got to be done, so you better not waste no time. The quicker*

119

you get up into the Uncompahgre country and find their hideout, the better.

Dropping both leather cases into the capacious side pocket of his coat, Longarm glanced around the saloon. Graves had bunched the men along the bar and was standing in front of them ready to restrain any of them who might try to get closer to the table where the shooting had erupted. Longarm walked over to the bar. The little group looked at him, most of their faces showing undisguised curiosity.

"I guess you've seen about all there is to see and heard all about who I am," he said. "But if you're still wondering, my name's Custis Long. I'm a deputy United States marshal, and I shot that fellow when he was going for his gun to kill me. I reckon there'll be some kind of hearing, but that's up to your own constable. He's in charge here now, and I'm going to leave and go to bed."

Before Graves or any of the others in front of the bar could speak, Longarm turned and pushed through the batwings. He walked to the corner and angled across the street to the rooming house. The hall lamp still glowed through the etched glass pane in the front door and gave him enough light to select the doorkey and find the keyhole. He opened the door and slipped quietly inside, locking the door behind him.

As Longarm straightened up and turned around he glimpsed movement at one side of the entry. Sweeping his Colt from its holster, he swivelled as he leveled the pistol. The landlady was standing framed in a doorway that led into a room off the foot of the staircase. She had on an ankle-length robe.

"My goodness!" she exclaimed. "Don't shoot me!"

Feeling a bit sheepish, Longarm let his gun hand drop, then quickly holstered the weapon. "I'm right sorry that I spooked you, ma'am. I sure didn't aim to, but you taken me by surprise."

"Well, I was all nerved-up myself," she replied. "I'm sure I heard some gunshots a little while ago, not long after you and your friend left. I came out here to the parlor to look out and see if I could find out anything."

"There was some shooting, all right," Longarm told her.

"But nothing that you'd be bothered about. It was over in the Stockman's Saloon."

"I was pretty sure it was," she nodded. "I've heard shots from there before." She looked past Longarm down the hall, and went on, "I didn't see your friend come back with you. Did he stay at the saloon?"

"I better set you straight about him," Longarm said. "He wasn't no friend of mine. The first time I ever seen him was this evening, on the Rock Island train coming up here. And he stayed at the saloon, all right, only it wasn't because he wanted to. He didn't have no choice. He's dead."

"Dead!" the landlady gasped. "Who shot him?"

"That's something else I better tell you. I did."

"You—you—" she stammered. "But the two of you seemed so friendly when you signed in here!"

"Things ain't always the way they look like, ma'am. We was polite to each other, not friendly. We shared a hack going from the Rock Island station to the Denver & Rio Grande. Like I told you when we rented the rooms, we was both trying to catch the train that runs up the spur to Creede."

"Yes, I remember you saying you'd missed it. But what's going to happen to you now? Won't the police come looking for you to arrest you? If they do, it'll give my house a real bad name, and I'm just making ends meet the way it is."

Longarm saw that he'd have to give her a more complete explanation. "You don't need to worry about that, ma'am. The town marshal came into the saloon just before the shooting. He turned out to be a man I knew in Denver. He used to be on the police force there."

"You certainly seem to know a lot of crooks and police-men, Mr. Long," Mrs. Bissel frowned. "I wonder if I—"

"Excuse me," Longarm broke in. "I ought've told you before now that I'm a sorta policeman myself. I'm a deputy U. S. marshal, outa the Denver office."

"Oh!" she gasped. "That certainly makes me feel better!"

"I figured it might," Longarm nodded. "Only I couldn't say nothing about what my job is while I was with that Anders fellow. I didn't know then that he was an outlaw, but I hadn't told him I'm a lawman, either. He tumbled to me while we

121

was in the saloon, and that's what set off the shooting."

"Well, I certainly feel better about everything now," she sighed. "And I'll say good night, then, and go up to bed myself, after I've had a cup of hot tea. If you'd care for one, it's as easy to brew a potful as it is a cup."

"Well, I thank you kindly, ma'am, but I got the heel of a bottle of whiskey in my saddlebags. I'll just have a swallow of it before I go to bed," Longarm told her. He touched the brim of his hat and bowed. "I'll bid you good night, ma'am."

"Good night, Marshal Long. I hope you sleep well."

In his room, Longarm shrugged out of his clothes quickly and sat down on the side of the bed wearing only his summer balbriggans. His saddlebags were within reach, and he took out the half-full bottle of Tom Moore which was wrapped in his spare gray flannel shirt. Swallowing a heartening tot of the sharp but mellow liquor, he lighted a fresh cheroot and took another small sip of the whiskey.

Puffing on the cigar, not yet sleepy enough to blow out the lamp, he remembered a chore he was about to overlook, and rummaged in the saddlebags again until he found the oilskin pouch in which he carried his gun-cleaning rag. Lifting his Colt from its holster, he pulled the oiled rag through its barrel, then began rubbing down the weapon. He was just getting ready to slide the gun back into its holster when a light tapping sounded at his door. Carrying the Colt, he padded in bare feet to the door.

Holding his voice to a whisper, he asked, "Who is it?"

"Just me, Marshal Long," Leila Bissel replied. "I hope you won't mind me asking a favor."

This was far from being the first such midnight summons Longarm had received. He said, "Wait till I get my pants on. It'll only take a minute."

Sliding into his trousers, he opened the door. As soon as it had opened wide enough, Leila Bissel slipped in. She was wearing the same long robe she'd had on while they talked in the hall, and she held a teacup in one hand.

Holding it out, she looked at Longarm, her height making her eyes almost level with his. "My cup of tea's not making me a bit sleepy, Marshal Long. Would you do me a favor and pour a little bit of whiskey in it?"

"Why, sure," he replied. "Just sit down—" He broke off and turned to watch her as she slipped past him quickly and sat down on the side of the bed, the cup extended toward him.

"I know I'm being forward," she told him, "but there are times when I do need a little bit of liquor to get to sleep."

"I'd imagine almost everybody has trouble going to sleep now and then," Longarm said, pulling the cork out of the bottle and pouring a generous tot of the Tom Moore into her teacup. He noted as he tilted the bottle that the cup was nearly empty.

"I do appreciate your kindness," Lelia said. She took two large swallows of the almost straight whiskey and nodded, then went on, "It's terrible when I can't go to sleep sometimes. A widow woman gets lonesomer than most others, I think."

"You been a widow long?"

"Four years. That's long enough to get used to the idea of being alone, I guess, but I do miss my late husband."

"Well, I guess I can see how you feel," Longarm nodded. He was still standing beside the bed, the whiskey bottle in his hand.

"Are you a married man, Marshal?"

"No, ma'am. I guess I never run into any lady that liked me enough to encourage me to propose to her."

"Well, now, I can't believe that!" Leila said. Her eyes were wide open and sparkling now as the whiskey began to work on her. "Why, I think you're a real handsome man."

"I thank you for your compliment, Miz Bissel—"

"Please," she broke in, "call me Leila."

"Leila, then," Longarm nodded. "And I got a sorta nickname my friends call me by. It's Longarm."

"Longarm," she said, emptying her cup with another swallow. "But you don't have to stand up. Why don't you come sit down by me?"

Longarm had felt himself beginning to stiffen during their conversation, and he moved at once to accept her invitation. As his weight pulled the mattress down, Leila lurched toward

123

him and he brought up his arms to catch her. She sank against him, the empty cup dropping to the carpet, her face upturned, offering her lips. Longarm bent to kiss her and as they held the kiss Leila's hand moved up his thigh to his crotch.

"Oh, my!" she sighed as their lips finally parted. "You're long in more than your arms! Do we have to play silly games any more, Longarm?"

"No," he answered, standing up and beginning to unbutton his balbriggans. "But I figured I'd just follow while you was leading the way."

Leila had risen when Longarm's fingers went to the buttons of his longjohns. She fingered the clasp at the neck of her robe and let it slip to the floor. She stood naked, the tips of the globes of her breasts puckered pink, her hips swelling above the shapely columns of her thighs, the golden fleece of her pubic brush glistening in the lamplight.

"Oh, my!" she gasped, throwing aside any further effort at pretense when she saw Longarm's jutting erection. "Hurry, Longarm! Take me to bed! You're the first man I've seen in a long time that's big enough to fill me!"

Chapter 13

Longarm woke at his usual time, opening his eyes and lying motionless while he stared up into the semi-darkness. Though the shade of the room's only window was drawn he could see the tinge of the slowly brightening sky beginning to trickle gray around the shade's edges.

He did not need the faint pungent aroma of perfume that reached his nostrils to remind him where he was. Turning his head, he looked at Leila Bissel lying beside him. She was still sleeping, her face framed on the pillow by the outspread ripples of her golden hair, the pink-tipped mounds of her high breasts rising and falling as she breathed. As Longarm moved his head she stirred. Her eyes opened, and she turned her head slowly to gaze at him.

"Have you been awake long?" she asked.

"No. Just for a minute or two."

"I'm sorry you woke up before I did," Leila went on. "I was going to wake you up in a special way."

"I ain't used to going back to sleep, once I've waked up," Longarm told her. "But if it'll pleasure you, I can close my eyes again."

"Do," she said. "Then just lie still. You'll know when it's time for you to move."

Longarm closed his eyes and lay quiet. In a moment he felt Leila's soft fingers riffling gently over the dark curls that matted his broad chest. Softly and slowly, its pressure feather-light, her hand moved down his body. Longarm did not move or open his eyes even when she kneeled on the mattress beside him and he felt the warmth of her breath on his skin as her lips followed the path her hand had traced.

Leila's wandering hand reached Longarm's crotch and he responded to the soft touches of her fingertips by swelling and growing erect as her caresses became more urgent. Then the moist warmth of her lips engulfed him and he felt her long hair brushing feather-light over his hips and thighs as her tongue began caressing him gently.

Longarm was lying with his arms stretched along his sides, looking down at her. Leila's face was partly veiled by the golden cascade of her long hair. Lifting one hand, Longarm cupped one of her swaying breasts in his palm and began rubbing its protruding tip with his iron-hard fingers. After a moment or two, Leila's body began to quiver. She did not slacken her attention to him, and as he continued to stroke and fondle her breasts he could feel small shudders running through her body now and then.

As the minutes ticked past, the frequency of her shivers increased, and soft involuntary moans bubbled occasionally from Leila's throat. Her body was shuddering constantly now, the quivers growing in their intensity until they built into spasmic undulations that shook her entire body. Leila released Longarm from the soft imprisonment of her lips and lifted herself above him, straddled his hips, and guided him into her. Longarm lay quietly. His only response was to bring up his free hand to fondle and stroke the pebbled tips of her swaying breasts as she rocked back and forth above him.

Leila's head was thrown back now, her long blond hair streaming down from her shoulders on both sides. She bent

126

forward, her hair falling forward in a golden cascade to form a tent that brushed Longarm's face and neck. The perfume of her body filled the canopy formed by her hair, filling Longarm's nostrils. Her hips were resting on his more heavily now, and as she twisted them from side to side Longarm began thrusting upward with his own hips in a counter-rhythm.

When he felt the weight of her body resting on him more and more heavily, Longarm knew that the time had come to increase the force of his upward thrusts. He brought his hips up to meet the fall of hers, going into her more deeply now. Leila cried out happily each time their bodies met. She threw her head back and began bucking and twisting. Longarm knew that her time of fulfillment was close. He grasped her hips again and held her pressed to him in his deepest penetration yet as he raised and dropped them, falling into the rhythm she had set.

Leila responded by bucking even more wildly. Her cries grew breathless and became throaty gasps, then finally with a loud cry she reached her climax and began tossing her hips and writhing uncontrollably. Longarm kept his firm hold, and continued his upward stroking with a faster and more vigorous rhythm until Leila's keening cries ended in a last spasmic scream and she fell forward on his chest, where she lay quivering and sighing contentedly.

Longarm lay motionless, too, still firm inside her, until Leila was quiet again. After a while she lifted her head and gazed down at him, then sighed and said, "This has been wonderful, Longarm. I'm going to hate to see you leave."

"Why, I ain't planning to leave till the train to Silverton pulls out, and that'll be late tonight," he told her. "Oh, I got a few little chores to tend to, but they can wait till later. Whenever you feel like it, we can start all over again."

When Longarm walked down Walsenberg's main street and turned to the neatly bricked walkway that led to the door of City Hall, the sun was beginning to take on the red-gold hue that marked the beginning of a Rocky Mountain sunset. A sign outside the doorway bore the word POLICE and an arrow pointing to the side of the building. Longarm rounded the end of the little structure and followed a somewhat tattered brick path to the rear, where he found a second door labelled POLICE and went inside.

Ed Graves, his hat pushed back on his head, sat at a rolltop desk, shuffling papers. He looked up when Longarm came in and said, "I was wondering if you was mad at me, Longarm, when you didn't show up before now. I guess I sorta messed things up for you last night."

"Oh, you done that, all right," Longarm agreed. "But you know I don't stay mad at my friends all that long."

"Sure. I remember how it used to be in Denver."

"What I come in for is to find out if there was anything in that Anders fellow's pockets that I might be interested in," Longarm went on. "I went through 'em in a hurry last night, but I wanted to get outa that place fast as I could. This case I'm on now's a mite ticklish, and I didn't wanta draw no more notice than I had to."

"I guess you looked in his purse and noticed all that cash he was carrying?"

Longarm nodded. "He had a pretty good load, but figuring he was a gambler and saloonkeeper, it wasn't too much."

"I wish I could afford to carry eagles and double-eagles like they was chicken feed," Graves said. "Why, there was over a thousand dollars in gold in that purse, and nearly two thousand more in greenbacks! It's a wonder he wasn't lop-sided from just toting it."

"That's about what I figured. It don't take many double-eagles to add up. I don't guess there was any brand-new ones amongst 'em?"

"I didn't notice any when I was counting his money so I could put how much he had on him in my report," Graves replied.

"You likely would've, if there'd been any," Longarm said. "I was thinking too about letters and stuff like that. I went through the suitcases he was carrying before I left the rooming house, but there wasn't anything in 'em but clothes."

Graves frowned thoughtfully for a moment and said, "Well, now, there was a little crumpled-up scrap of paper in his vest pocket. It had some scribbles on it, but as far as I could tell they didn't mean much."

"Maybe not to you, but I might get a lead out of 'em. Do you remember anything at all what they were about?"

"Like I said, they wasn't anything but hen tracks. Just a name or two and some days."

"Days?"

"Sure, Tuesday or Thursday or maybe Wednesday. I didn't see that they meant much."

"What'd you do with it?"

"Why, I put it back in his pocket after I looked at it. I guess it's still there."

"Where's that vest?" Longarm asked. "If you don't remember what was written on it, I'd like to see it."

"I guess it's still on him, unless the undertaker's got around to fixing his body up by now. I got Frank Smithy down at the undertaking parlor to pick him up and take care of him."

"His body'll be at the undertaker's, then?"

"Sure," Graves nodded. "Frank'll embalm it and box it up, if he ain't done that already. Then if nobody claims it inside of a week or two, he'll bury it, like his contract with the city calls for."

"I better get a look at that paper, Ed," Longarm said. "Where's this undertaking parlor at?"

"Just off Main Street, a couple of streets west. If you want me to, I'll walk down there with you and show you."

"That might not be a bad idea," Longarm nodded. "Whenever you get through with what you're doing."

"Oh, what I been working on ain't all that pressing," Graves said. "I'll catch up on it sooner or later."

A cool evening breeze was wafting down from the western peaks, gilded now with the beginning of the long high-altitude sunset, as the two men strolled down the quiet street. As Graves had promised, the walk was a short one. He stopped in front of a building that seems to suffer from a dual identity. On one side of it a sign read SMITHY'S FURNITURE STORE and on the other a second sign read F.SMITHY, UNDERTAKER.

"This is the place," Graves said. "And it looks like Frank ain't closed up yet."

129

As they entered the building, crowded with furniture on one side of a partition which cut off about a third of the floor space, a chubby middle-aged man came to greet them.

"Frank, this is U. S. Marshal Long, from Denver," Graves said. "He wants to take a look at the body you got from the Stockman's last night."

"Why, sure," the furniture dealer and undertaker replied. "I got him laid out and all fixed up. Come on along."

Longarm and Graves followed the man into the partitioned side of the store. The curtains which veiled the front window and the lack of any others reduced the light in the room to a dim twilight. A cloth-draped bier occupied the front area. On it stood a closed coffin. Smithy pushed the lid to one side, displaying Anders's body. The dead man's face was paler than it had been when he was alive, as were his thick-fingered hands clasped neatly across his chest to cover but not quite hide the blood that stained his coat.

"I didn't put him in a burying suit," Smith said. He turned to Ed Graves and went on, "But I can later, if his kin want me to. I didn't want to charge a suit to the city, even if you did say he had enough money on him to pay for an A-one laying away and a funeral, if nobody shows up to claim him."

"Just like we always do," Graves nodded. "I sent a wire to that saloon he's got in Albuquerque. I imagine we'll hear from them by tomorrow. If we don't, you can put him away here."

"I'll do whatever you say," Smithy told Graves. "But you know what I'm up against in cases like this. A lot of the time, men that get killed the way he was don't have any family to claim them, and for what the city pays me to handle these bodies, I can't afford to waste good merchandise."

"Now that you two've settled up your business, I need to do a little bit more than just look at him," Longarm told Smithy. "What I'm after is a piece of paper that he had in one of his pockets."

"His vest pocket," Graves broke in. "I saw it last night before you picked him up, and I put it back where I'd found it."

"Then all you need is his vest," Smithy nodded. "I didn't

130

put it back on him. No use wasting time that way, you know. His vest is hanging up on that rack over there."

Leading Longarm and Graves to a rack that contained a motley assortment of garments, Smithy fingered along the row and pulled out the vest. He handed it to Longarm, who probed into one bottom pocket, then the other, and brought out a crumpled, tattered scrap of paper.

When Longarm smoothed out the paper into an inch-wide strip, he could see that it had obviously been torn from a large sheet, for while the ends were smooth the top and bottom of the strip were ragged. There were two lines of pencilled writing on the strip, the cramped script smudged and dim. Holding it to the light that trickled around the drapes of the window, he could barely make out what was written on it.

...*from Walsenberg to Silverton* the note read *there a man will meet you. You must to him your coin show and he then will bring you to Telluride and beyond to our new place which is* ...

Longarm lowered the strip of paper and stood frowning at it, then tucked it into his pocket and turned to Graves. "Looks like this is what I sorta figured it might be. And that's all I need. Come on, Ed. Let's you and me go get some supper. I'm getting a mite hungry by now. We can talk about this while we eat."

Darkness had fallen almost completely by the time they left the undertaking parlor and started back toward City Hall. As they walked down the street and came to the city offices, Graves said to Longarm, "There's a boardinghouse just two or three doors down that sets a real good table. They don't have nothing but coffee to drink, but if you feel like a sip or two—"

"I'm a lot hungrier than I am thirsty," Longarm replied. "Let's go to this place and get some supper. I know you got night rounds to make, and I got to go pick up my gear at the rooming house where I stayed last night."

"Well, you got all the time in the world." Graves pointed ahead of them to a low rambling building. "There's the boardinghouse I was talking about. It don't look like much, but they set about the best table in town."

Just past the short entrance hall of the boardinghouse, Graves led Longarm into a large room almost filled by a U-shaped table, spread with a checked cloth and lined on both sides of its perimeter with plates and cutlery. They sat down, and within minutes a chubby, rosy-faced woman brought a tray on which rested a platter of sliced roast beef, bowls of boiled greens and red beans and potatoes, and a plate of smoking-hot biscuits.

"I guess you've got a busy night ahead, Ed, you're here so early," she said, distributing the food in front of them as she spoke. "You and your friend eat hearty, now."

"You put his dinner on my bill, if you don't mind," Graves told her.

"Not a bit. Now, I'll get on back to the kitchen. I've got a little more work to do before the rush starts."

"We don't have to hurry," Graves told Longarm as he began passing platters and bowls. "The train going up the Silverton spur don't pull out till late."

"Oh, I ain't feeling pressed for time right now," Longarm said. "But a lot of what I'm going by is just guesswork."

"As I recall, you was always a pretty good guesser."

"Maybe so. But I'd rather be sure about what I'm going to run into."

"Trouble, unless you've changed a lot since we worked those cases together in Denver."

"There's sure to be some," Longarm agreed.

"You were going to catch me up on this case you're on," Graves reminded Longarm.

"I don't know enough about it myself to tell you much, Ed. All I got is a suspicion that there's a new gang getting organized up in the Uncompahgre country, and I got to do all I can to bust it up before it gets started."

"Well, there's been gangs before, and none of 'em has lasted very long. The James boys, Jack Slade's boys, and that outfit nobody knows much about that hid all that gold on the Higgins place, and the Jim Reynolds bunch up at Leadville, and Coe's crew down at Trinidad."

"Sure," Longarm nodded. "But all of them was mostly pickup bunches that didn't have any kind of real organization.

132

This new outfit I figure to be forming up does."

"Well, whatever and whoever you're after, I'd say you feel a lot better about getting onto 'em than you did a little while ago," Graves went on. "I guess whatever was on that piece of paper in the dead man's pocket gave you some kind of lead."

"Well, it did if I read it right," Longarm replied. "And I guess it makes sense. Except I'd feel a lot better if I had a little bit more to go on."

"You don't reckon you'll get it?"

"Not with everybody I know who could give it to me being dead. Including one of our deputies outa Fort Smith. I dug up his body down on the Ute reservation quite a while back, and I've been backtracking to find out where he'd been before he got killed. That's what brought me here."

"I didn't know about that, Longarm, or I wouldn't've pushed in on you and that fellow last night."

"That don't matter a lot right now, Ed. You more'n made up for it by helping me today. I got a hunch that paper I got outa Anders's pocket's going to get me where I need to be."

"Which is where, Longarm?"

"Damned if I know for sure. All I'm real certain about is what I'll be doing later on tonight."

"What's that?" Graves asked.

"I got to get on tonight's train up to Silverton. This piece of paper was torn out of a letter, it's easy to see that. It says somebody'll be waiting for this Anders fellow at rail-end. I take that to mean they wasn't sure when he'd get there, so whoever is supposed to meet him will likely still be waiting, if I get there quick enough. And I sure don't aim to lallygag around and miss 'em."

Longarm woke on the green plush seat of the accommodation car and peered through the window, looking back at the thin gray line which marked the beginning dawn. He was now the lone passenger in the coach, but there'd been only two others when the train left Walsenberg, cavalrymen who'd gotten off at Fort Garland.

Though the train ride would have been short if measured by a bird-line, winding tracks and the darkness had made it seem to last forever. He'd lost track of the number of times the train had stopped in the almost impenetrable gloom to cut off empty ore cars at the sidings leading to mines that were invisible from the train. Except at two or three stops where the distant flicker of light marked a mine shaft, the sidings had been dark, deserted except for loaded ore-cars waiting to be picked up by the train on its return journey.

From Alamosa, where Longarm had started his earlier trip, the tracks curved sharply north and the engine had begun to labor as it started the steep pull up the flanks of the Rockies. The stops to drop off empties had begun in the foothills at Del Norte and from there the grade had increased and the frequency of the stops had multiplied as the mines grew more numerous.

Ahead, the whistle blasted the stillness. Longarm turned to the window again. A few faint lights flickered ahead, and the train was already beginning to slow down. In a few more moments the lights resolved into lanterns hanging on shacks beside the right-of-way, the gleams of the lanterns expanded into halos as they spread out in circles along the unpainted boards on the walls where they'd been hung.

A few dark figures became visible in the gloom as the train came to a stop with the grinding of brakes. Longarm picked up his gear, already assembled and waiting at the back of the coach. His saddlebags in one hand, his rifle in the other, his bedroll over one shoulder, he stepped off the coach.

From the shadows that made a pool of blackness between the two railroad shacks, a man stepped forward into the small pool of light. He stopped for a moment, looking at Longarm, then came closer.

"You're looking for somebody to meet you here?" he asked.

"I sure am," Longarm replied. "Are you him?"

"You don't see nobody else, do you?" the man countered.

"Now that you mention it, I don't."

"We'll get started, then. But first I got to make sure you're who you say you are. Pass it over and let me take a look at it."

Chapter 14

For a moment, the man's abrupt demand left Longarm puzzled, then he realized that the request could mean only one thing. Lowering his saddlebags to the ground, Longarm dug into his pocket. Then the realization of his predicament came to him as he felt the two leather packets. He had no way of knowing which of the twin squares contained the double-eagle Anders had shown him when they first met.

Old son, you better have Lady Luck setting on your shoulder this time, he told himself silently. *You sure as hell can't take out both of them gold pieces and pick out the right one, and if you give this fellow the wrong one all hell could bust loose the minute he looks at it.*

There was no way he could see to resolve the puzzle. Longarm selected one of the packets and handed it to the stranger without looking at the coin inside.

Nodding, the man stepped over to the nearest lantern. Longarm caught the glint of gold as he watched him take out the coin and hold it in the lantern-light. He glanced at it, shook his head, brought it closer to his eyes, and shook his head again. Then he stepped back to Longarm and held out the coin.

"Even if that damn lantern didn't give me enough light to read the number, the snake was plain enough, so I seen all I needed to. Come on. I left the horses tethered over there by the ore-pile."

Suppressing the sigh of relief he felt like letting out, Longarm put the double-eagle back into the leather packet and returned it to his pocket before he asked, "How far have we got to ride?"

"Over the hump to Telluride and on past it a ways."

Longarm shook his head. "I don't know this country as good as I might. How far does that make it?"

"Far enough," his guide said curtly, as they reached two horses tethered beside one of the ore-piles to a switch-lantern that glowed red in the diminishing darkness. "You take the paint pony. The dapple's got my saddle on it."

Both horses were saddled, but even in the gloom Longarm had no trouble distinguishing the paint horse from the dapple. He threw his saddlebags over the horse's rump and tied them in place, then levered himself into the saddle. The outlaw was ready to ride first, and sat waiting until Longarm mounted. He geed his horse ahead and Longarm followed, keeping the nose of his horse a little ahead of the dapple's rump.

They rode on past the train, its crew busy beside the tracks, dark shadows moving between the sidings lined with ore-cars waiting to be coupled to the string. Beams of yellow light shot through the pre-dawn darkness as the brakemen waved their lanterns in signals to the engineer, and the short hoarse wail of the locomotive whistle pierced the night as their signals were acknowledged.

Wheel-flanges screeched on the tracks now and then when the locomotive crossed a switch moving to another siding, and occasionally all the lesser noises were overriden by a loud harsh clang when couplers met as an ore-car was joined to the engine or the lengthening string that was taking shape on the main line.

Silverton began where the railroad tracks ended. It was a one-street town, a mixture of residences and stores lining its only street. Patches of light spilled out across the dusty thoroughfare from the batwings of saloons, the yellow gleams emphasizing the deep ruts cut by ore-wagons from the mines beyond the town.

As they reached the first of the buildings, Longarm's outlaw guide reined his mount as close as possible to the ragged line of buildings on one side of the street, to keep their horses from tripping on the ruts, and Longarm followed his example. As they passed through each patch of light, Longarm devoted himself to taking stock of the man riding beside him.

He was a lanky man, and even in the intermittent light Longarm could see that his seamed face had been tanned as brown as the backs of his gloveless hands. His nose had met too many fists and showed it; its nostrils were flattened and its bridge broken into a series of small humps. His eyes were such a light blue that they were almost colorless, and peered like a blind man's between stubby lashes. His jaw was wide, his cheeks scarred and pitted from smallpox. His lips were thin, just a line that cut the vertical seams on his upper lip. A two-day stubble covered his cheeks and chin.

They'd gone about halfway through Silverton when the outlaw turned to Longarm and asked, "I don't guess you got a bottle, have you?"

"I got one," Longarm said. "But there ain't much left in it. I guess we can buy one here or in Telluride, can't we?"

"Hell, you don't even want to go inside a saloon or even look at one when you're here or in Telluride, either. The nearest place hereabouts where one of us dasts to belly up to a bar is Alamosa. The boss has got his own ideas about a man taking a drink."

"You mean he figures we might spill something if we take one or two too many?" Longarm asked.

"That's about the size of it."

"I guess we better kill this bottle I got before we're too close to him, then."

"Oh, once we get to the hideout you don't have anything to worry about," the other man said. "The boss hands whiskey around real free, and you can drink any amount you can hold."

They rode on in silence to the end of the deserted street, where the houses of Silverton thinned down to a few scattered shanties. When the trail out of town forked the outlaw turned his mount onto the path leading north. After they had covered a half-mile, the lights of the locomotive and the lanterns of its crew had faded. Above them the sky was slowly changing. On the downslope to their right it showed the soft gray glow that appears before sunrise, while on the left it still held night's deep blue punctured by bright stars.

They had gone only a short distance along the upslanting trail when Longarm toed his horse ahead and brought himself even with his guide.

"About what I asked you a while back," he said. "You mind telling me how far is far enough?"

"It'll take us the rest of the day, and we won't be getting there till after dark, on account of the going's pretty rough sometimes. You don't have to worry about riding hungry, though. I got grub for both of us in my saddlebags."

"I've got some, too," Longarm said. "It's mostly jerky and parched corn, but with what you've got I guess we'll be all right."

"Sure," the other man nodded.

"I didn't catch your name," Longarm went on. "But maybe that's because you didn't mention it."

"Well, now I'm sure about who you are, I don't guess it's going to hurt none to tell you. Call me Tracy." He was silent for a moment, then added, "I guess you don't know yet about us not calling our names outside of the valley."

"I reckon that's because I'm new. I didn't ask to look at your double-eagle, either."

"I figured out why. Hell, I ain't got used to this rigmarole about numbers and double-eagles and all that myself. But I guess it'll come along after a while."

"I imagine," Longarm agreed. Then, to fit himself more solidly into his role as an outlaw like his companion, he went on, "But mostly it seems like a pretty smart idea. I don't know

138

as I'd say as much for the idea about cutting us off from having a drink, though."

"What I was telling you you ain't as bad as you taken it. He don't say a word if we step up to the bar unless it's real close to where we're going on a job. But once we get nearby where we're heading for, it's another story. You don't even wanta smell a cork if we're getting ready to go to work."

"Seems to me like he oughta make up his mind," Longarm commented.

"He don't have a bit of trouble doing that. You'll find out, after you been around a little while. Matter of fact, you're likely to catch him on a rough edge when we get there."

"Why's that?"

"You was due to get here yesterday. He don't take kindly to any of us not showing up right on the dot when we're meeting somebody."

"I missed connections in Walsenberg," Longarm explained. "Got to the depot just about a minute after the train pulled out. I figured whoever was supposed to meet me here would wait, so I wasn't too worried."

Tracy shook his head. "That yarn wouldn't cut much ice with the boss."

"You got any idea why he's so persnickety?"

"I can't say for sure, but I heard a story about it," Tracy replied. "The way I heard it, him and Jim McKinney was headed out to collect whatever they could from a bank down in Arizona, and Jim took a mite too much aboard."

Tracy paused for breath and Longarm said, "I heard about Jim McKinney a time or two. Whatever happened to him?"

"That's what I'm getting to," Tracy answered, a tinge of impatience in his voice. "Jim drawn his gun while they was still on the street in front of the bank. One of the town marshals seen him and cut down on 'em before they got inside. Well, they got McKinney, but the boss dived out the back door and managed to give 'em the slip. The thing is, he never has forgot how near he come to winding up on boot hill with Jim."

"Well, thanks for letting me in on the way things is," Longarm said. "I'll keep what you said in mind."

"Don't go asking a lot of questions when we get there,

either," Tracy cautioned. "That's something else the boss don't like."

"Sounds like he's got a lot more don'ts than do's," Longarm commented. "I ain't too sure about how I'll like it, having somebody order me around all the time."

"That's how I felt, right at first," Tracy nodded.

"And you changed your mind? I'd like to know why."

"That ain't a hard one. I seen how I can stick with this scheme the boss has come up with for just two or three years. Then I aim to knock off and go live comfortable anyplace I want to. What I figure to do is settle down maybe out in California, where I ain't got no wanted circulars to worry about. I do that, and I won't ever have to face a lawman with a gun pointed at me again, or maybe try to get away from a hanging posse. No, sir! This is one outfit I ain't about to quit."

"I got to admit you got a point there," Longarm nodded. He was beginning to get an idea of what the man Tracy called "the boss," and whose real or assumed name Longarm still didn't know, had in mind for the gang he was organizing. "I know how edgy a fellow gets looking out through bars."

"Edgy, hell!" Tracy exclaimed. "I been in jail a time or two, just like most of us has. I'd sure liked to've had somebody outside that'd come break me free."

Armed now with the first real clue he'd picked up since Vail had assigned him to the case, Longarm could respond quickly.

"I guess anybody that's spent time in jail thinks about that," he said.

"There's a lot more to the boss's scheme that maybe you ain't learned," the outlaw went on. "Any of us is liable to take a bullet or some shotgun slugs, and this hideout we're going to is so far from anyplace else it'll give us a safe place to hide out till we've got healed up. That's worth a lot to a man on the run."

Longarm had spent many years hunting down men on the run, and knew perhaps even better than the outlaws did themselves the value of a safe haven waiting for a crook trying to elude the lawmen searching for him. Tracy's remarks had now given him the answers to a number of the questions he'd been asking himself since he first stumbled onto the new gang's existence. He now had a reasonably good idea of the kind of case his search for Jim Houlihan's killer had turned into.

"I'll sure have to put in with you there," he agreed. "But I'd hate to have to make it up here from just about anyplace if I was carrying a chunk of lead under my skin."

"I guess you ain't heard yet about all the things the boss has got figured out," Tracy said. "Let's see. If I recall rightly, he said your place is in Albuquerque."

Longarm remembered his assumed identity in time to nod and say, "That's right."

"Then you won't be seeing much of the hideout again, not unless you get into trouble down in New Mexico Territory. But you'll be seeing the boss now and again, and anybody from our bunch that needs a hidey-hole to duck into."

Faced with improvising again, but anxious to keep his companion talking, Longarm said, "I don't suppose you'd know how many more hidey-holes the boss has got fixed up by now? He never did tell me."

"It ain't likely he would, so early in the game. And he keeps on fixing up new ones, like yours is going to be. The closest one we got to the south now is in Tucson, or maybe the one down in Abilene is closer. But both of them is a long ride from here."

"Hell, anyplace you go in Texas is a long ride from any-place else," Longarm said.

"That's where you're from? Texas? If you are, you sure don't talk like it."

"No, siree," Longarm answered. Seeing no harm in dealing with facts for a change, he went on, "I come outa the hard scrabble country, West Virginia."

"You got any special thing you do best, like banks or trains or stagecoaches?"

"Well, now, that'd be my business, wouldn't it?" Longarm countered. Then, seeing that his questions might lead him onto ice that was even thinner than was now underfoot, he went on, "I guess I better put a stopper in my mouth before I get to talking too much."

"Now, the boss'd like that, I can tell you!" Tracy nodded. "And if you wanta do me a favor, just don't let on like you heard anything about what I been telling you. The boss likes to pass all this on to a new man hisself."

Longarm took the opportunity to cover in advance some of the mistakes he might make in the future. He said, "All he told me was how much money I stand to make by going in with you men."

"Oh, he'll pass the rest of it on to you soon as he feels like it. I don't know much myself, except that he picked you out to fix up a place we can use for a hideout in Albuquerque, whenever we need it."

Wondering more than ever now about how long he could sustain his role, Longarm said, "He give me a pretty good idea about what he's got in mind. But don't worry, Tracy. I know as well as the next man how to keep my jaws from flapping."

Tracy only grunted in response. Then he toed his horse ahead, taking advantage of a stretch where the trail narrowed to ride in the lead.

Don't push your luck, old son, Longarm told himself as he looked at the back of his guide. *Just tag along behind and keep your jaws from flapping so much. The less you say, the better off you'll be. You make any kind of slip-up in the yarn you got to spin these outlaws, and your name's gonna be spelt different. It'll be just three little letters, M-U-D, mud.*

Twisting in the unfamiliar saddle, Longarm tried to ease the dull ache that had started in his buttocks while they had been making slow, uneven progress along the narrowing trail that wound in zigzags up the sloping sides of the central spur of the Rocky Mountains. The crest of the range was just ahead now, and the sun was dipping toward the tips of the tallest peaks.

Since starting from Silverton, they'd made only one stop longer than the few minutes required to rest their horses from the constant ascent up the trail that had grown constantly steeper. At Telluride they'd halted long enough to go into a saloon for a drink and a visit to the free lunch table, but during

142

most of the short stops made to let the horses breathe they hadn't even dismounted. It seemed to Longarm that the longer they'd been on the trail, the more anxious Tracy had seemed to push ahead.

By now signs of mining activity had almost vanished. There were fewer treeless areas here than on the lower slopes of the Uncompahgres. In the area they'd already traversed the piles of stony earth furrowed by rain and melting snow that marked abandoned claims had been plentiful. After leaving Telluride the signs of prospecting had been fewer, and now had vanished completely.

Before they reached the line of shadow cast by the setting sun which since late afternoon had been creeping up the pine-covered slopes to meet them, Tracy had remained silent. He'd continued to ride in the lead on the narrow trail, and now they had reached a height where they could look down into narrow valleys at the tops of the trees which grew at lower levels. Only a half-dozen peaks towered above them now, gilded by the reddening rays of sunset.

Even before leaving Telluride Longarm had given up trying to make conversation, for the air was thin at the altitude at which they travelled. In spite of frequent rest stops their horses had moved more and more slowly as they traversed the long, steep slope on the zigzagging trail. Except for the whistle of the animals as they breathed the thin air and an occasional rustle from the trees, the silence of the seedling pine forest was almost total in the chilling high-altitude air.

Longarm broke the silence. "You got any idea how high we've climbed by now?"

"Plenty high," Tracy answered. "It's right around ten or eleven thousand feet at Lizard Head Pass up ahead. At least that's what the boss told me when I rode this way with him the first time."

"How much farther we got to go?"

"We'll tilt downwards after we get through the pass, and the rest of the way's mostly downhill. That don't mean the going's much easier, so if we don't push ahead now, it'll be way after dark before we get to headquarters."

Tracy nudged his horse ahead, taking the lead again on the

narrow trail. Longarm followed, and for the next mile or more they rode silently. They were in a narrow defile where the massive stone walls that rose on both sides towered high above their heads when Tracy reined in so abruptly that Longarm's mount bumped the outlaw's horse.

"What's wrong?" Longarm asked.

"Somebody's ahead," Tracy replied. He whipped his rifle from its saddle scabbard and sat holding it, ready to shoulder it. "I don't know who, but I don't aim to get caught napping."

By now the clatter of hooves on the stone-hard ground was echoing off the narrow walls. Tracy sat motionless, holding his rifle by the throat of its stock. When the head of the horse ridden by the approaching rider showed around a jog in the narrow crevasse he raised the weapon, ready to shoulder it. Then he saw the rider and lowered the gun.

"We got nothing to worry about," he told Longarm over his shoulder. "That's one of our men. Grizzly Pete."

Chapter 15

"I was sorta figuring you'd pop up along the trail," the new-comer said as he reined in just short of bumping into the outlaw. "The boss told me to keep an eye out for you. I guess this is the hombre you was supposed to get there yesterday with?"

Tracy nodded, then said, "He'd missed his train at Walsen-berg, Griz. That's why I didn't get back when I was supposed to. It ain't my fault or his, either."

Both men had been ignoring Longarm. He decided to break in on their conversation, hoping he might pick up some help-ful information. He said to the new arrival, "I hope your boss ain't too mad about me being late, but like Tracy said, missing that train wasn't something I'd figured on."

"Oh, he ain't likely to tear into you. Fact is, he's too sick to raise much of a ruckus, even if he was inclined to," Grizzly Pete replied.

"Sick?" Tracy frowned. "What's wrong with him?"

"Well, now, if anybody knowed that, I wouldn't be going after a doctor, would I?" Pete countered. "All I know is, he got me outa bed before sunup and asked me did I have any yarbs that was good for the belly-gripe. I brewed up some tea outa dry willow leaves and assifidity, but it didn't help him none, so he told me to hit out for Telluride and bring back the sawbones."

"You'd better be getting along, then," Tracy suggested.

"Reckon I had, at that," Grizzly Pete nodded. "You be sure to tell him you run into me."

"Sure," Tracy nodded. He turned in the saddle to watch the old man for a moment as his horse carried him up the steep trail, then said to Longarm, "We better keep moving, too. We're late enough getting back as it is."

They moved ahead down the winding trail, and as their slow progress continued the character of their surroundings gradually changed. Shelving rock formations and towering boulders gave way to the greenery of shrubs. Then trees began to replace the low brush, and finally they were again riding through thick stands of pines.

Now the trail was no longer narrow, its twists grew less sinuous. Then the pines began to thin and suddenly stopped abruptly. Below them a broad valley spread, a gently sloping mountain meadow covered with high green grass stretching away from the trail. Here and there the grass thinned to show glints of water from a small stream that wound through it. A mile or so distant, Longarm could see a wisp of gray smoke rising against the sky.

"Looks to me like we must be getting close to where we're heading for," he remarked, nodding toward the smoke-trace.

"You got pretty good eyes," Tracy said. "That's where we're going, all right."

"Even if I can't tell much about it, far as we are from getting there, it looks pretty good to me," Longarm told his companion. "My belly thinks my throat's been cut, and all I wanta feel under my butt for a while now is a chair."

"You don't exactly ride like you and horses are strangers," Tracy commented. "If the boss hadn't told me different, I'd

146

take you for a man that put in his time running a cattle spread instead of a saloon."

"Oh, I ain't always been in the line of work I am now," Longarm answered quickly, realizing that Tracy was much more observant than he'd given the outlaw credit for being. "I done my share on the range before I got smart and figured my time was worth more'n a dollar a day."

"I guess it takes a while for some of us to come around to it," Tracy nodded. "But I figured that out, too. That's when I quit cowpunching and threw in with some fellows I'd run into and held up my first train."

While he was still talking, the outlaw reined off the path and headed across the meadow. Longarm followed him at once, looking for a trail through the wavy wisping grass, but seeing none.

"Looks to me like you're in a real hurry to get there," he commented.

"No more so than usual. We ain't supposed to ride across the meadow in the same place every time. The boss figured it wasn't smart to make a trail to the camp. He said it'd just invite anybody that come along to ride over and stop in for a visit."

"You know, this boss you keep talking about must be a pretty smart fellow," Longarm went on.

"Well, he must've struck you as being smart when you talked to him. If he hadn't've, you wouldn't've come all this way from Albuquerque to get your deal smoothed out."

"I didn't mark him as being short on brains," Longarm said quickly.

Realizing that he'd been very close to making a mistake by talking too much, he pulled out a cigar and clamped it in his teeth as he reined in his horse to let the outlaw get a short distance ahead of him while he struck a match and lighted it. Tracy looked back once when Longarm fell behind, saw him with his hands cupped in front of his face, and turned around and continued toward the outlaw headquarters.

Longarm took his time catching up with Tracy, his mind busy trying to form a plan that would keep his identity hidden as long as possible. He'd considered two or three schemes and discarded all of them, and was still trying to form one when the buildings of the hideaway took shape and form as they drew closer.

From the trail, the big log main house and a rambling barn had not been visible. Neither had the pole corral that stood beside the barn. A half-dozen horses lazed in the corral. The entire outfit had been invisible from the trail, concealed by a screening growth of tall old pines and young aspens.

As they drew closer, Longarm could also see several smaller structures for the first time, small cabins that stood away from the main house. He counted them quickly, and realized at once that he had been underestimating the number of outlaws he might have to face.

There were six cabins, and only two showed signs that they'd been there long enough to have been a part of the original spread which the outlaw gang had taken over for their hideout. The wide-planked walls of the four remaining cabins were still as yellow as they'd been when the boards came from the sawmill, and though these had been spaced widely apart, scattered out in a stand of mature trees, their sides glared with the bright glow of freshly sawn lumber.

Looks like you finally got where you been heading for, old son, Longarm told himself silently as he rode to catch up with Tracy. *And if all them shanties has got outlaws in 'em, you just might've bit off a bite that's going to be a mite hard to chew. If Gunge Peyton's in one of them shanties, he's going to yell our right away, and even if he ain't there's likely to be some damn outlaw or other that'll know you from a case you've worked on before. But there sure ain't no way of turning around and backing out even if you wanted to. You got yourself into this. Now it's going to be up to you to figure a way out.*

Spurring his horse, he caught up with Tracy and asked, "I guess we'll start out by talking to the boss, won't we?"

"Sure. And if you're wondering when we'll be ready to catch up on our shuteye, he won't talk much. But I'd imagine that's going to depend on how he's feeling by now."

They were within a few hundred yards of the big house now. Longarm saw a man sitting on a bench on the wide

148

veranda that ran across the front of the rambling structure. He looked at the man closely, and was thankful that he did not recognize him.

"That's Big Joe on the porch," Tracy said. "Him and me are sorta straw-bosses. I'd guess the boss is still ailing, or he'd likely be outside with Joe."

As Tracy reined up at the hitchrail, the man on the veranda stood up and came over to the steps. He carried his rifle with him. Longarm reined in beside Tracy's horse, but instead of dismounting when his guide did he remained in his saddle.

"Finally got back, did you?" Big Joe said to Tracy. "You sure taken your time. The boss has been growling like a sick bear, wondering what the hell happened to you."

"Grizzly Pete told us he was ailing," Tracy replied. "We run into him on the trail just a little ways out from Telluride. How's the boss feeling now?"

"Not too good. Says his gut feels like he's all swole up inside, and he can't hardly stand up."

"You reckon he'll perk up enough to talk to us when I take this new fellow in?"

Big Joe shook his head. "Don't try going in at all. The boss told me to stay out here and see that nobody bothered him until Griz gets back here with the doctor."

"What do you expect me to do with him, then?" Tracy asked, jerking his thumb over his shoulder in Longarm's direction.

"Find him a place to bunk down," Big Joe said. "I guess you seen his double-eagle before you started out?"

"Damn it, Joe, I ain't a plumb fool!" Tracy replied. "Sure I did!"

Longarm breathed an inaudible sigh of relief at the respite he'd just been given. Even an hour or two would give him time to come up with some kind of plan that might enable him to survive the discovery of his real identity. He'd survived too many encounters with outlaws to have any false ideas about them, especially the kind of veteran lawbreakers that the mysterious man all of the gang called "boss" seemed to attract.

He said to Tracy, "As long as the boss knows we've got here, I don't see much need to be in any hurry. When you come right down to it, I could do with a little bit of shuteye about now, myself. If you'll just tell me where to spread my bedroll, I'll have a little snooze and talk to the boss later on, when he's feeling better."

"That makes sense," Tracy nodded. "I don't guess I've had any more sleep than you have, and a little while in my bunk oughta make me fitter to be around." He turned back to Big Joe and asked, "Did the boss say where he wants this new fellow to bunk?"

"No, but I suppose we've got enough brains between us to figure something out," Joe replied. "There ain't but two shacks where there's a bunk empty. He can go in with Grizzly Pete and Twistnose or with me and Scotty. We'll have a spare bunk in our cabin, at least till Gunge gets back from wherever it is he's gone to."

Although Longarm's expression did not change to give either outlaw a hint that he'd recognized Gunge Peyton's name, he spoke up quickly, before Tracy had a chance to offer an opinion. At the same time, his mind was busy weighing the chance he'd have of coming unscathed out of the trouble Peyton would trigger off the instant Jim Houlihan's killer returned to the outlaw hideout and recognized Longarm.

Looking at Big Joe, he said, "I ain't persnickety about where I put down my bedroll, but if I go into your place and that fellow you said was gone gets back soon, I'd just have to move out anyways. If it's all the same, I'll save trouble and take the one I won't have to move out of."

"That makes sense," Big Joe agreed. "I'll tell the boss you've got here, and if he wants to talk to you he'll know where to look for you."

"Come on, then," Tracy told Longarm. "I'll show you which one of the cabins it is. And if you're as tired as I am, you're ready to crawl between your blankets for a little while before supper."

"There ain't no need for you to put yourself out no more on my account, Tracy," Longarm said. "Just point out which one it is and I'll settle in by myself. I guess nobody's going to object if I put this nag in the corral?"

"Go ahead," Tracy nodded. He pointed to one of the

weatherbeaten cabins. "It's that one," he said. "And the shit-house is in that clump of baby aspen over there to the left of it. Tell Twistnose that—"

"No need to worry about Twistnose," Big Joe broke in. "He went out a while back to see if he could spook up a deer. We're getting short of meat."

"Well, I'll tell him why I'm here when he comes in," Longarm volunteered. "He ain't a hard man to talk to, is he?"

"Not when he's sober," Tracy said. "And it ain't likely he taken a bottle with him, if he went hunting meat."

"I'll be getting over to the cabin, then," Longarm nodded. "I reckon one of you'll come after me when the boss feels like talking?"

"Don't worry," Big Joe replied, "you'll know. The boss ain't a man to wait, either, so when he sends word for you to come over and talk, you'd best shake a leg."

"I'll keep that in mind," Longarm told the outlaw. He felt the eyes of the two men on his back as he turned and walked toward his horse. Freeing the reins from the hitchrail, he led the animal to the cabin where he dropped his saddlebags, rifle, and bedroll on the ground. He led the horse to the corral and began unsaddling it. While he worked, his hands almost automatically unbuckling the saddle straps, he noticed that the little stream he'd glimpsed from time to time during the trip from Telluride had been diverted into a ditch to carry a flow of water along one side of the enclosure.

After tossing the saddle gear on the top rail of the corral fence and turning the horse in with the half-dozen others, he started walking slowly back to the cabin, surveying the house and cabins and the area surrounding them. The big depression in which the ranch was located was well-grassed, but in spite of its size it was dwarfed by the mountains that rose all around it. As big as the saucer was, it would not provide enough graze to support a large herd of cattle, even during the short high-altitude summer.

Thinking back over the trip he and Tracy had made from Telluride, Longarm could remember having passed no other large area of meadow that could provide summer pasture for a cattle herd of any size, nor did what he'd seen since arriving at the hideout give any indication that the place had even been substantially different in size.

From the looks of the outlaws' headquarters, it had at one time been either a small cattle ranch or had served as summer range for a big spread. There was no windmill, not surprising at an altitude where winter winds blew fiercely, nor was there any sign that the place had ever supported a bunkhouse or the corrals and outbuildings which would have been needed for the men required to handle a large herd. Nor had he seen enough open country on the way there from Telluride to support extensive grazing.

Whoever picked this place up for an outlaw hideout sure did luck out, he told himself silently. *Or maybe he was just smart enough to look around till he found what he was after. But that ain't here nor there. You got yourself in between a rock and hard place when you come here, old son, even if you did find out that Gunge Peyton's going to show up here sometime pretty soon. And from the way them outlaws has been talking, it appears like that fellow they always call the boss acts a lot like you'd expect Rattler Reyna might, if what you heard about him's true.*

So maybe you got a pretty good hand, if you just pick up an ace or two when the time comes to draw. Only trouble with that is, you might be setting in a game where the deck's already stacked against you. Whichever way it is, you're going to have to do some pretty good bluffing if you figure to be on top when the time to call comes around.

When Longarm reached the cabin, he pushed the door partly open and peered around its edge at the inside of the cabin. The single room was dim in contrast to the bright sunshine outdoors, and he stood blinking for a moment. All he could see was the bright glowing glare from the single window set in the wall opposite the door. The glare filled his eyes, but he could make out the small stove standing just inside the door and the bunk that stood below the sun-filled window.

As his eyes grew accustomed to the changed light Longarm saw the other two bunks which with the one below the window took up most of the cabin's floor space. The bunks on the

152

end walls plus the one below the window in the back wall filled most of the limited space of the little rectangular room. Longarm pushed the door open a bit wider and the rusty hinges grated. On the bunk to his right, what he'd taken to be a huddle of blankets moved and stirred and a man's head emerged from the blankets.

"Griz?" the man mumbled, his voice still blurred with sleep. "You sure made a hell of a quick—" He stopped short and sat up, blinking at Longarm, and went on, "You ain't Griz. I guess you'd be the new fella the boss has been so riled about for not gettin' here fast enough to suit him."

"That's right," Longarm agreed.

"He's talked about you comin' up here, but the only thing I heard him call you is 'that fella from Albuquerque.' I guess you come looking for that empty bunk over yonder?"

"I sure did," Longarm nodded. "I ain't had enough shuteye to go between a gnat's hind legs the past couple of nights."

"I guess you got a name, ain't you?"

"Sure," Longarm replied. "Except the fellow that brought me up here said the boss didn't cotton to us calling names."

"Well, he don't. When he wants one of us for something, he generally just points and says 'hey, you.' But he don't mind if we call each other by the names we go by, them we've picked up."

Throwing back his blankets, the outlaw got up from the cot and stepped over to the window. In the light that came through the streaked, dusty pane, Longarm saw that his nose was a grotesque lump of flattened and deformed tissue that obviously had been broken and smashed more than once.

"You don't have to do more'n look at me to figure what the handle is I travel under," the man said. "And it don't hurt my feelings a bit when folks calls me Twistnose."

Longarm saw that he must exchange names with Twistnose to keep from offending him. He followed his custom of using his own first name in situations of the kind he now faced and said, "I answer to Custis as good as I do to anything else."

"Well, you come in here to get some sleep," Twistnose said. "Nobody's using this bunk, so spread your bedroll and lay down on it and welcome. The other one belongs to Grizzly Pete, and he's gone to Telluride to get a doctor for the boss."

"I know," Longarm nodded. "Me and Tracy run into him on the trail while we was coming up here."

"I don't reckon the boss feels no better?"

"I couldn't say," Longarm replied. "All I found out was that he's pretty sick."

"Well, now I'm up and around, I guess I'll mosey over and find out," Twistnose said. He walked out of the cabin and started toward the main house.

Longarm wasted little time in bringing in his gear. The bunk was bare of bedding. It had no pillow, and only a thin mattress covered its board bottom, but it was a bed of sorts, and he knew that sleep was what he needed more than a feather mattress. He spread his blankets over the soiled mattress and shed his coat, then folded it to use as a pillow. Sitting down on the bunk, he levered out of his boots, took his Colt out of its holster, and placed it where his hand could reach the butt instantly. Then he stretched out.

This bed ain't such a much, old son, he told himself silently as he wriggled to find the most comfortable spot on the thin lumpy cotton that filled the mattress. *But you've slept on a lot worse, and it sure beats bare ground. Now all you got to do is figure out how to keep your skin from getting shot full of holes when you wake up and these outlaws tumble to who you are.*

Before he could even begin to shape a plan for action, the fatigue he'd been accumulating for the past several days caught up with him. Longarm's eyes closed and he fell asleep.

Chapter 16

When the scratching of a match broke the cabin's silence, Longarm awoke instantly. As always when he'd been aroused from even the deepest slumber, his senses were instantly alert and his reactions as fast as though he'd been up and on the go for hours. During the few seconds that passed while he was kicking aside his blankets and getting up from beneath them his hand went to the butt of his Colt and the revolver was leveled at the match-flame before his feet hit the floor.

"Hold on there!" Tracy's now-familiar voice exclaimed. "You ain't got nothing to worry about as long as you're here among friends!"

Longarm let the Colt's muzzle sag in his hand as he replied, "I guess it's a habit I got when I get roused up in the dark outa a sound sleep, but before *I* bust in on a fella, I generally call out and let him know I ain't coming in shooting."

"I didn't stop to think about how new you are here," Tracy

replied. "I guess it's mostly my fault. Anyhow, there's no harm done."

Holstering his Colt, Longarm said, "Oh, I'd've made sure who you was before I triggered."

"Well, that makes me feel better," Tracy told him. Before he could go on, the match he was holding began flickering and the outlaw blew it out. "I came up to see if you was ready to eat some breakfast."

"You mean it's tomorrow already?"

"It sure as hell is. It'll be daylight inside of another hour or so. Twistnose and me has been sitting out on the porch over at the boss's house waiting for the doctor."

"I don't guess he's got here yet?"

"Grizzly Pete rode in with him just a few minutes ago."

"What'd the doctor find out?"

"He hasn't said, yet," Tracy replied. "He didn't waste much time popping into the boss's bedroom to look him over. Then he come back out and told us he wasn't about to guess at anything and that he'd tell us what was wrong as soon as he'd had a better look."

"I guess we'll find out pretty soon, then." Longarm paused long enough to strike a match and touch its flame to the tip of the cheroot he'd fished out while Tracy was talking, then added, "I didn't aim to upset you, Tracy, throwing down on you like I did, but you taken me by surprise."

"I guess I ought've knocked before I opened the door," Tracy said. "But I'll give you this, you had me looking down the barrel of your Colt quicker than I ever saw a man do it before."

"Oh, that wasn't such a much. It was right to my hand by my pillow. When I turned in, I didn't figure to fall away and sleep all night," Longarm told the outlaw. "But what you said about breakfast sure sounds good. I'm so hungry my belly thinks my throat's been cut."

"Well, Big Joe said he was sleepier than he was hungry and left to turn in a few minutes after Grizzly and the doctor got here. Twistnose and Griz was hungry, and so am I, so they're frying up some bacon and spuds. There's a big skilletful of 'em, so I figured you might like to have a bite with us."

"I'd take that real kindly," Longarm told the outlaw. "Just give me a minute to slide my feet into my boots."

Walking beside Tracy through the darkness toward the big house, Longarm looked around. Except for the lights that spilled out of the headquarters house and a thin, luminous rectangle that outlined the door of one cabin, the remainder of the cabins were dark.

"It sure don't look to me like you got a lot of men staying here," Longarm commented. "Course, I ain't had time yet to look around much or to meet up with anybody but you and Big Joe and Twistnose. Oh, yes, and that Grizzly Pete fellow we run into on the trail."

"Well, nobody's going to get rich staying here," Tracy said. "Let's see, now. The Mexicans take up two cabins, and all of them are down in the Texas Panhandle. They aim to get a herd together from what they can cut out of the big spreads down there. That'd count out six of us. Gunge Peyton's been gone a week now on some kinda job he's got cooked up. Scotty ain't here much. He likes to go out in the mountains and shoot deer. Soto's off spreeing, getting rid of whatever he got out of the last train job he was in on. So that just leaves me and Grizzly and Twistnose and Big Joe and Barclay and Parks and Smith and Scotty and Fletcher here."

"And the boss," Longarm added.

"Oh, sure," Tracy agreed.

"I ain't run into some of them fellows yet," Longarm said, frowning. "They keep to theirselves, or what?"

"Well, Fletcher's new, and none of us except the boss knows much about him," Tracy answered. "Parks and Smith's sorta standoffish, they keep to theirselves a lot, but I reckon that's their own business. Barclay says they get him edgy when he's around 'em, and that he'll be glad when they pull out for another job."

"How about Barclay?"

"He's all right. Don't have much to say, but he's a good man with the horses. Spends most of his time at the barn and the corral."

While Tracy talked, Longarm had been making a mental tally to find out the odds against him. Without giving his

157

words any emphasis to indicate that his interest was more than the idle curiosity which would be expected of a newcomer to the hideout, he remarked, "I'd say nine's a pretty good bunch. Like you just said, a man's got to get out and work at his trade if he's going to make anything."

"Nine don't stack up to how many the boss says we'll likely have pretty soon. He figures there'll be two or three times as many here at one time soon as this scheme he's got starts working out. I ain't so sure I'm going to like it then, with the place so crowded up, but I aim to give it a try for a while."

By now they had reached the main house. A lantern was hanging above its doorway now and the horses ridden by Grizzly Pete and the doctor stood in front of the building at the hitchrail. The front door stood open, light from it spilling out to mix with the glow of the lantern. Longarm followed Tracy inside and found himself in a long room that spanned the entire front of the house. Three doors filled the opposite wall, two of them open.

Grizzly Pete and a stranger stood beside the long table that spanned the center of the room to divide it roughly into halves. The newcomer was a young man. His forehead was high, his brown hair slicked back in a long pompadour that glistened with macassar oil. His beard was thin and straggling, its sparseness emphasizing the youthfulness of his face instead of adding the maturity its wearer intended. The moustache above the beard was equally thin. He had on a dark suit with a coat cut long, and a puffy black bow tie above a stiffly starched dickey that was bulging and creased.

"Looks like the boss has got something real serious," Pete told Longarm and Tracy as they came in. Frowning, he turned to the man beside him. "What in tunket was it you called whatever it is, Doc?"

"Perforating inflammation of the vermiform appendix," the doctor replied. Seeing the puzzled frowns on the faces of Tracy and Longarm, he went on, "Folks outside the medical profession are beginning to call it appendicitis, because that's the portion of the anatomy afflicted."

"Maybe you can tell us what all that fancy language

means," Tracy suggested. "All we thought the boss had was a gut-ache."

"Why, the vermiform appendix is a little sort of bag that dangles down from a man's main gut, to put it in the language most folks use," the doctor said. "It gets infected now and then, and unless the infection's serious, all it causes is a stomachache."

"What the boss has got is the serious kind," Grizzly broke in when the doctor paused. "Seems like he could die of it if that appendix thing ain't cut out of him."

"That's correct," The doctor nodded. "The inflammation is poisoning his entire body. And I'm preparing to perform an operation as soon as your boss is unconscious. I've just given him a dose of laudanum, and he'll be sleeping so soundly in a few more minutes that he won't feel a thing."

"Well, I guess you know better'n us what you need to do, Doc," Grizzly said. "And I ain't going to argufy with you."

"Thank you, Mr. Pete," the doctor nodded. "Now, there's one thing that I'm concerned about. Judging by the conversation I had with him, he seems to be worried about one of his men, Tracy's his name. Would that be one of you?"

"That's me, Doc," Tracy volunteered. "I been away on a job he sent me out on, and I guess he's wondering if I got back all right."

"Perhaps you'd better step into his room and assure him that you're all right, then," the doctor suggested. "There hasn't been enough time for the laudanum to put him to sleep, and it's my belief that the patient will stand the shock of the operation better if his mind is free from worry."

"Seems to me he'd be worrying enough about being cut open," Grizzly snorted.

"Exactly," the doctor nodded. "That's why I suggest that Mr. Tracy step in and demonstrate that he's arrived safely."

"Hold on, Doc!" Tracy protested. "Suppose I catch this appodzix or whatever it is he's got?"

"I assure you, there's no danger of that, Mr. Tracy," the doctor replied. "What your employer suffers from is not infectious. You can be in the same room with him—in the same bed, for that matter—without any danger."

159

"Well, I'll go tell him I got back all right, then," Tracy nodded. He took a step toward the door of the room where the leader of the gang was lying, then turned and said to Longarm, "Maybe you better step in with me. If he was to see that I got you here all right, it'd likely soothe him more'n if I just told him you was here."

Before Longarm could object, the doctor said, "A very good idea! Go ahead, Mr. . . . I don't know your name, but if Mr. Tracy was supposed to escort you here and your employer has been worried about both of you arriving, it would probably be very beneficial to his condition to see both of you. Do by all means go with Mr. Tracy."

With Grizzly Pete and Tracy both watching him, Longarm saw that the danger of letting the boss glimpse him was likely to be less damaging to his plans than risking a refusal. He was also aware that he'd never gotten a glimpse of the gang's leader, and he wanted to be be able to identify him later on. Shielding himself as much as possible without making his intentions obvious to the others, he stepped behind Tracy and followed him into the room.

A glance was all Longarm need to tell him that what had seemed a good idea was only effort wasted. The man lying on the bed had a towel swathed around his head and a loose bandage wrapped around the bottom of his face. A sheet covered his body from toe to neck. All that Longarm could see of the outlaw leader was a pair of obsidian eyes, almost obscured by their drooping lids, and the man was obviously having trouble focusing them on him and Tracy.

"Here's that fellow you sent me to get, boss," Tracy said quickly. "I'd've had him here sooner, but he missed his train in Walsenberg and I had to wait over an extra night in Silverton. But you see we got here all right. You can quit fretting about us."

For a moment the sick man's slitted eyes shifted toward Longarm. Then he spoke in an almost inaudible whisper, muffled by the bandage that covered his mouth and chin as well as by the effects of the opiate the doctor had given him. The sheet that covered him stirred as he tried to lift his arms, but the laudanum he'd been given was taking effect swiftly, and his movements were nothing more than futile gestures.

"You reckon he knows who he's looking at?" Tracy whispered to Longarm.

"Seems like he recognized you," Longarm replied. "But he's just about to go under. Maybe he'll sleep better for seeing you, though."

By now the boss's eyes were completely closed. Tracy looked down at his sheet-covered figure for a moment, glimpsed the shining steel surgical instruments lying on a small table beside the bed, and shook his head.

"Them things give me the shivers," he said in a half-whisper. "And the boss is out cold now. Let's you and me get the hell outa here before that sawbones starts carving."

Longarm was as ready as Tracy to leave the sickbed. He followed the outlaw into the long narrow room where Grizzly Pete, Twistnose, and the doctor waited.

"How'd he look to you?" Grizzly asked Tracy.

"Sleepy as hell. I reckon he seen us, all right, but I ain't too sure he knew who we was."

"Seems to me he recognized you," Longarm said, trying to hide the relief he felt. "But I ain't sure he knew who I was." Then, in keeping with the role he'd assumed, he added quickly, "Course, he'd only seen me one time before, and we didn't talk together all that long."

"Well, he'll be fully conscious late tomorrow—or perhaps I should say tonight," the doctor put in, looking at the wood-cased clock that stood above the fireplace. "Now, if you gentlemen will excuse me, I have to get started with the operation. The effects of the laudanum will wear off unless I hurry."

As the doctor left the room, Twistnose said to none of them in particular, "I don't know about you boys, but I'm ready for breakfast. Come on, let's get to the grub before them hotcakes gets too soggy."

Seated around the kitchen table, the four men ate without talking except to ask for a platter to be handed around again. They'd finished eating and were getting ready to leave the table when the doctor stepped into the room.

"You done finished, Doc?" Grizzly Pete asked.

"Oh, yes. The operation's really a very simple one. A small incision, snipping off the appendix, then—"

"You don't have to tell us all about it," Grizzly broke in. "We all figure you know what you're doing. I reckon you're going to stick around till the boss wakes up, ain't you? We can fix you up with some breakfast, and if you want to catch some shuteye there's a room next to the one the boss uses that's got a bed in it."

Shaking his head, the doctor replied, "No, thank you. I appreciate your offer, but there will be patients coming to my office who'll need my attention."

"Suppose the boss gets worse?" Grizzly asked.

"I'm sure he'll make a good recovery," the doctor replied. "But he can't move out of his bed for at least a week. I'll come back then and remove the stitches. If he should develop a fever, one of you can ride in to Telluride and get me."

"You're the doctor," Tracy said. "I guess you know best."

"I'm sure that I do. Now, about my fee—"

"You tell me how much it is and I'll pay you on the spot," Grizzly broke in. He dug a long, thin purse out of his jeans and opened it. "The boss can pay me back when he's better."

"I'm afraid I'll have to charge twenty dollars," the doctor said. "The trip out here, the surgical supplies, and—"

"There ain't no need for you to explain," Grizzly interrupted. "All any of us cares about is that you come out here when you was needed."

He dumped the contents of the purse into one hand. Most of the coins which fell into his palm were gold pieces, though there were a few silver dollars and some small change. Longarm also saw that among the coins there was one of the square leather packets like those in his own pocket, which contained the double-eagles the gang used for identifying its members. Grizzly picked two of the eagles out of the mixture of coins and handed them to the doctor.

"You done a good job," he said. "And we thank you for it. We'll look after the boss all right till you come back."

When the doctor opened the door to leave, Longarm saw that the blackness of night was giving way to dawn's grayness. The sun had not yet started rising, but the peaks of the high mountains west of the crater-like valley that sheltered the outlaw hideout made a dark jagged line against the leaden sky. Across the clearing in which the hideout huddled, he could now make out the squared shapes of the cabins and the barn, and see the dark figures of the horses shifting slowly around in the corral.

Before the doctor could close the door, Longarm noticed a man come out of one of the cabins near the corral and start toward the main house. He stopped and watched the approaching figure. The light was too dim for him to see the man's face and there was nothing in his stance or walk which was familiar. Longarm's first thought was to start back to the cabin where he was staying, but after a moment he decided that he'd have to get acquainted with all the men in the gang. Knowing how each of them might be expected to act in a showdown was the best insurance he could have. He stayed in the doorway and waited for the man to reach the main house.

As the stranger drew closer and saw Longarm, he kept his eyes on the doorway. Longarm was sure the new arrival was studying him, just as he was studying the other man. A few more steps brought him close enough for Longarm to make out his features. There was nothing distinctive about them. The new arrival was of medium height, and Longarm's concern was relieved when he could see the man's face clearly and tell that he was not numbered among the lawbreakers he'd encountered in the past. The stranger was young, rawboned, and needed a shave. Dark stubble a half-inch long covered his cheeks and jaws.

Before the new arrival was within speaking distance, Tracy came up to join Longarm in the doorway. He looked at the man and said, "That's Scotty. You ain't run into him yet, I guess."

"First time I've seen him," Longarm agreed.

"He's all right. Don't say much, and don't stay close to the place when he's here. Like I said, he's off hunting a lot of the time."

By now Scotty was within easy speaking distance. He said, "When I got back from my deer hunt, Big Joe told me the boss is sick. I'd've come over here then, but I was just about

163

dead beat after lugging the forked horn I shot all the way back. How's he doing?"

"Pretty good, I guess," Tracy answered. "He ain't waked up yet from whatever medicine the sawbones give him to put him asleep while he was cutting him open, but it looks like he's going to be all right." He turned to Longarm and went on, "This here's Scotty. Scotty, this is Custis, the fellow the boss sent me to get down at Walsenberg."

Scotty did not offer to shake hands. He was taking a closer look at Longarm than had been possible in the gloom and the distance. At last he nodded. "How do, Custis. I got to say, you don't look much like what I'd figured you would when the boss was talking about you a few days ago. I don't recall seeing any barkeep before now that didn't run to fat."

"Some do, some don't, I guess," Longarm replied. "Like they say, it takes all kinds."

"I hope there's enough grub left for me to have a bite of breakfast," Scotty went on.

"I guess there'll be plenty to fill you up," Tracy said. "Even if we didn't put your name in the pot when we was cooking it up."

"You'd better put another name in the pot while you're at it," Scotty said. "And maybe cook up a little bit more besides, because the camp's heavy eater rode in while I was out by the barn gutting out that deer I shot."

Chuckling, Tracy said, "I don't have to guess who you're talking about, Scotty."

"Nobody else would, either," Scotty told him. "There ain't one of us that can stow grub away like Gunge Peyton."

Chapter 17

Longarm's mind had started flashing danger signals the instant he heard Gunge Peyton's name, but his face betrayed nothing of his feelings and he kept his voice carefully casual.

"Seeing as I ain't all that much of a cook," he said, "I guess the best help I can give you is to keep outa the way. I'll just mosey back to the cabin."

"Don't go on my account," Scotty told him.

"Oh, I ain't," Longarm said. "But hearing you talk about deer hunting give me an idea. I ain't had time to do none for quite a spell. I might just go for a little ramble through them trees and see if I can still hit a deer myself."

"If you're going to hunt this morning, you'd better get started," Scotty said. "Another hour or so and the big bucks will be bedding down for the day."

"Just what I was thinking myself," Longarm nodded. "But I don't reckon I'll be out very long. The country hereabouts is all strange to me, and I got sense enough not to go far enough so's I'd get lost."

"Good luck to you, then," Scotty nodded. He turned to Tracy and went on, "Now, since you said there's not much grub left, I'd better go get some breakfast before somebody else shows up hungry and beats me to it."

As Tracy and Scotty started toward the door, Longarm headed for the cabin where he'd spent the night. He took his time as he walked across the clearing in the brightening dawnlight, knowing that at any moment he might encounter Gunge Peyton, who would be sure to recognize him in an instant.

Safely inside the cabin and reasonably sure that neither Grizzly Pete nor Twistnose would be leaving the main house soon, Longarm sat down on his bunk and lighted a cigar.

Old son, he told himself, *you've had luck looking over your shoulder so far, but your string's just about to play out. Right this minute you're caught tight, right in between a rock and a hard place.*

Soon as he sees you, Gunge Peyton's going to start yelling out who you really are. Then you ain't got no choice but to take on the whole damn bunch at once, and that's about the time when your string's going to give out. The best thing you can do is to drop outa sight and hole up till it gets dark. Maybe by then you can come up with a scheme to snag the whole kit and kaboodle and figure out a way to get 'em behind bars where they belong.

Longarm wasted no time in putting his half-formed plan into action. He'd pushed his saddlebags under his bunk before turning in the night before. Now he dragged them out and opened them. Opening the drawstring of one of the soft leather bags in which he carried his spare ammunition, he counted the rifle shells carefully. There were eleven. The second pouch held the loads for his Colt, a total of eighteen, and four of the stubby .44 caliber bullets for his derringer.

You ain't going to run short unless you do a lot of wild shooting, that's one thing sure, he assured himself as he replaced the ammunition pouches in the saddlebags. *But if you ain't real careful to play every card you got just right, you're sure gonna be up shit creek without a paddle.*

166

Tossing the saddlebags over his shoulder and picking up his rifle, Longarm left the cabin. When he stepped outside and saw that the cleared area ringed by the corral and the cabins and the headquarters house was deserted, he stood for a moment surveying the high mountain peaks that towered above the clearing. There were three of them, one to the north, one almost due east, and the third to the south.

Looking west, he could see no peaks in the immediate area, though through the early morning haze he could see in the distance peaks even higher than those which rose around the outlaw hideout. On the east side of the clearing four cabins and the horse corral as well as the headquarters building were all potential danger points. To the west he'd have only two cabins to pass before he reached where the forest thickened.

If you was to try to get outa here on a horse, it'd take ten or fifteen minutes to saddle up, and that's too long, he told himself. *The best thing for you to do is head for them trees on the west and get outa sight in a hurry.*

Shifting his load as he moved to get his saddlebags balanced on one shoulder and carrying his rifle by the throat of its stock, Longarm started walking west. Ahead of him only two of the cabins stood between him and the sheltering undergrowth that grew belly-high between the tall pines of the dense forest. He had covered half the distance to the first cabin when its door swung open and a man stepped out.

As soon as Longarm had seen the door start to open he'd lowered his head to shield his face with his hatbrim. He knew he had no choice but to pass uncomfortably close to the man coming out of the cabin. To have turned and retreated or changed his course and swung wide to avoid passing close to him would have been the same thing as standing up on a soapbox and announcing that he was trying to get away without drawing attention.

"Headed for a deer, I see," the man in the cabin door said as Longarm drew closer to him. "I guess—" He stopped abruptly and the tone of his voice changed from one of greeting to one of sudden suspicion. He went on, "Wait a minute! I knows you from some—" He fell silent for a split second, then shouted, "Longarm!"

In the fraction of a second that had lapsed between the beginning of the man's fraternal greeting and his shout of recognition, Longarm had recognized both his face and his voice. The man was Gunge Peyton.

As he called Longarm's name, Peyton's hand was sweeping to his holstered revolver, but Longarm had recognized the outlaw with his first glimpse of Peyton's face. Without stopping to shoulder the rifle in his hand, he brought up the muzzle and triggered it from his hip.

Peyton's voice was cut off a fraction of a second after he'd called Longarm's name, but his loud greeting and the crack of the rifle would have aroused even the soundest sleeper.

Before Longarm had time to take more than a step from the spot where he'd triggered the rifle, before the echoes of his fatal shot had died away, even before Peyton's body reached the ground, crumpling in death, the outlaw's pistol still in its holster, Big Joe appeared in the doorway. He had a pistol in his hand, but Longarm gave him no chance to level it and fire.

On seeing Big Joe, Longarm realized he would have too little time to lever a fresh shell into the Winchester's chamber. He let the rifle fall and swept his hand up as the weapon dropped, grabbed his Colt from its holster, and fired as he swung it toward the outlaw.

While the shot he loosed at Big Joe was half-aimed and half-instinctive, it went home, but did not have the pinpoint accuracy of the rifle shot. The bullet took the outlaw just below the point of his shoulder, tearing into the collarbone joint. The shock of the slug threw the bulky outlaw back into the cabin and left him sprawling on the floor, bellowing in pain. He lost his grip on his revolver as he toppled backward, and the weapon fell to the ground outside the cabin door.

Longarm did not wait to see how badly he'd wounded Big Joe. He knew the outlaws in the other cabins as well as those in the main house would respond to the firing within seconds. Scooping up his rifle, Longarm headed on a run for the cover of the pine forest, still forty or fifty yards away.

Excited voices raised at the main house were filling the air in the clearing before Longarm reached the shelter of the trees. He paid no attention to the cries, knowing that several minutes must pass before the renegades in the gang's head-quarters could reach the cabin and find out what had happened. He reached the first line of tall-standing pines and continued running toward the brush that stood ahead.

Shouts and cries still sounded from the main house when Longarm dodged between the massive boles of the pine trees. With each minute that passed, their volume grew louder and he could hear the voices of the men rushing toward the cabin more clearly as they came closer. Longarm glanced over his shoulder without slackening his pace. He could see the running outlaws more clearly now, and if he had had the breath to spare would have loosed a sigh of relief, for not one of them carried a rifle.

Longarm had passed the narrow belt where only the great pines grew and was getting close to the underbrush-covered ground long before the outlaws reached the cabin and stopped to cluster around Big Joe. He was too far away to hear them clearly, but once heard the outlaw he'd wounded call his name in an angry and unusually loud shout.

Before the men who'd clustered around Joe in front of the cabin broke up and spread out, starting toward the pines, Longarm had pushed his way deeply into the thick stand of gooseberry bushes that grew to a height of five or six feet and covered almost every inch of ground between the trunks of the pines. His saddlebags had slipped from his shoulder down to his elbow, forcing him to bring up his arm and crook the elbow, then fight the tangling branches out of the way to keep from losing the bags entirely.

When he finally came to a halt in the brush thicket, he was breathing hard. He dropped to one knee and let the saddlebags slip to the ground. Flexing his arm to stretch his cramped muscles, Longarm planted his rifle butt on the ground and leaned on it while he waited for his breathing to settle down into its usual steady automatic rhythm instead of gulping gasps caught on the run.

In his improvised hiding place he could hear the calls of the outlaws clearly, as well as the rustles of disturbed brush around him as they extended their search into the stand of pines. The nearness of the search sounds jogged Longarm's memory. He opened the saddlebag in which he carried his ammunition and found the bag containing shells for the rifle. Pulling out a handful, he dropped all but one into the pocket of his coat, slid the shell he'd held back into the magazine of his Winchester, then took out the bag of pistol ammunition and replaced the spent shell in the Colt's cylinder.

Longarm's breathing had settled down to normal now. He had heard no noises to indicate that any of the men searching for him were close by when a voice that seemed to be speaking only inches from his ear froze him into total immobility.

"He's gotta be someplace around here. He ain't had time to get very far," the speaker panted.

Longarm recognized Twistnose's nasal tones. His voice sounded as though the outlaw was only inches distant.

"He don't need to be very far in this damn brush," another outlaw replied. His voice was strange to Longarm. The man went on, "Thick as these bushes is, that damn lawman could be where we could touch him if we could just see him."

This voice was strange to Longarm. He remained motionless, though the temptation to stretch out belly-down on the ground was strong. Having learned from his early gunfights as a lawman the disadvantages of such a position, Longarm did not move.

Twistnose said, "He could, at that, but I bet he ain't. He's likely circled back to the trail. My bet is he's still running. It's too bad these bushes is so green. If they was dry, we could burn the bastard out."

"Now, that's an idee!" his companion exclaimed. "The bush don't have to be dry! We can set fire to the duff!"

"Ah, come on, Barclay!" Twistnose scoffed. "Where'd you ever git an idee like that?"

"When I was lumberjacking out in the high Sierras. I wasn't but a lard-ass kid then, but I sure found out that these dry pine needles on the ground will burn. They don't make much fire unless there's a pretty good wind, but there's enough of a one right now to spread a fire like I'm talking about. These pine needles will smoke up the woods so thick and strong a man can die if he breathes in too much of it."

"Damn it, you sound so positive I almost believe you!"

"You better believe me, Twistnose," Barclay replied, his voice level but convincing. "I know what I've seen with my own two eyes out in the Sierras. All we need to do is get a fire started, and we'll flush out that bastard Longarm!"

"You think coal-oil will burn hot enough to start the kinda fire you're talking about?"

"Sure. Coal-oil, lard drippings, high-proof liquor, or just about anything that burns hot and fast'll set it off."

"We got a fresh barrel of coal-oil up in the barn," Twistnose said thoughtfully. "I reckon that's plenty to start a pretty good fire."

"Sure," Barclay agreed. "I can't think of a thing that'd be much better."

"Then let's circle around till we find Grizzly Pete," Twistnose said. "Or Tracy, if we run across him first. Them two is sorta straw-bosses when the real boss is gone, and him being laid up like he is, I guess they'd have the say-so about trying out your scheme."

Longarm heard the brush rustling as Twistnose and Barclay started away. The shouts of the other outlaws were distant now as they fanned out farther and farther in the search. He waited until rustling noises of Twistnose and Barclay had died away before he moved himself. Moving slowly and carefully, parting the undergrowth ahead of him with the barrel of his Winchester to avoid making the telltale rustles that would give away his position, Longarm started edging slowly and carefully back toward the clearing.

You got a real job on your hands now, he told himself silently as he moved. *There's seven of them fellows out here looking for you, and if they get a chance to start them fires the two of 'em was talking about, you ain't going to have no hidey-hole to dive into. Looks like they really got you with your pants all the way down to your boot tops this time.*

Suddenly the sober thoughts that were racing through Longarm's mind came together and developed into a full-blown idea.

Now, if them outlaws goes along with that scheme Twistnose and that other fellow was trying to hatch up, they ain't going to be able to bunch up together, he considered. *They'll have to split up to set them fires they figure on using to make you come out where they can get at you. And when they get separated that way, it won't be seven on one no longer. It'll be man to man, and that kinda changes things. One on one is odds you don't need to back away from.*

He worked his way closer to the edge of the pine stand and found a spot where the low-hanging bottom boughs of a late-growth pine brushed the tops of the chest-high gooseberry bushes. The pine was at the edge of the clearing, and when he crouched beneath it and peered out through the small slit between the bottom limbs of the pine he could see along the entire perimeter of the circular clearing.

Hunkering down, Longarm found that he had an almost unhampered view from the headquarters house on his left to the corral and barn and the wide-spaced cabins on his right as well as along the edge of the pine forest. Dropping to one knee and leaning on his rifle, he made himself as comfortable as possible and prepared to wait.

His wait was not a long one. Only a few minutes ticked off before the first members of the gang emerged from the cover of the trees and started across the clearing. Longarm recognized Tracy at once, but the man with him was an outlaw Longarm had not seen before. Though the distance was too great for him to hear what the two were saying, it was obvious that they were arguing.

They started angling across the clearing toward the barn, but had taken only a few steps before a shout from the opposite side stopped them. Longarm turned quickly and saw that Grizzly Pete and Scotty had now emerged from the stand of trees.

"Hold up," Grizzly Pete called to Tracy. "We better do a lot more talking before we start going about that crazy scheme Twistnose and Barclay's pulled outa their hats!"

"Let's get closer together, then," Tracy shouted in reply. "I ain't gonna stand here all day braying like a mule!"

Tracy and his companion started walking toward Grizzly Pete and Scotty, while the latter pair moved to meet them. The four came together almost directly in front of Longarm's hiding place. When they spoke, he found that he could hear them clearly.

As the outlaws stopped, Grizzly Pete said angrily, "Where in hell did you get such a fool idea, Tracy?"

"Now, hold up!" Tracy protested. "From what Twistnose told me, I figured you was the one that dreamed up this scheme to smoke Longarm out!"

"Damned if it was me!" Grizzly retorted. "I didn't have a thing to do with it!"

"Twistnose was lying, then," Tracy frowned. "Now why the hell would he do a fool thing like that?"

"Because he figures we oughta put him in with me and you, taking charge of things when the boss is off someplace else," Grizzly answered. "Oh, I seen him looking at us and getting sorta green around the gills when we tell him or one of the other fellows to do something."

In spite of the dangerous spot he was in, Longarm's lips twitched in a half-smile. What he was hearing was an old story to him—the jealousy of one outlaw in a gang toward another. He noted Twistnose as one of the soft spots he might use to drive a wedge between the renegades if he managed to get out of his present predicament unscathed. When Tracy spoke again, he turned his full attention back to the four outlaws.

Tracy was shaking his head. He said, "Looks like you and me need to have a talk with Twistnose. But we'll have to put it off till we run down that sneaky son of a bitch Longarm."

Scotty spoke unexpectedly. "That scheme Twistnose has come up with might not be as crazy as it sounds, Tracy. I think it'd work, if we go about it right."

"Suppose you tell us why you think it'll work," Tracy suggested. "It still sounds like a damn fool notion to me."

"I don't guess you've ever been out in California," Scotty said. "I have. I've lumberjacked out there in those mountains and I've seen how that duff under pine trees burns and spreads. All it needs is a good start."

"You figure coal-oil will start it all right?" Grizzly asked.

"Sure," Scotty nodded. "All we'd have to do is light up a line of fire so the wind will blow it in the right direction. It'll make a big stinking smoke when it spreads along the ground and anybody holed up in there will come out pretty damn fast."

"Here comes Twistnose and Barclay now," Grizzly Pete broke in. "I tell you what, Tracy, it won't do no harm to give that smoking-out scheme a try. We could prowl through them trees all day and all night and never spook out Longarm."

"If you say try it, I'm agreeable, too," Tracy nodded. "Let's see, Parks and Smith's the only ones that ain't here yet. They're up to the north of here someplace and it won't be such a much of a job to get 'em. Fletcher, you prowl up where they started and tell 'em to come out fast."

As Fletcher started toward the line of pines, Twistnose and Barclay came up to join the other outlaws.

"Now, about this scheme of mine," Twistnose said. "We got almost a full barrel of coal-oil up in the—"

"Save your wind, Twistnose," Grizzly Pete broke in. "We been standing here hashing over that scheme you and Barclay come up with, and we figure it's worth a try."

"I'll stay here and wait for Fletcher to come back with the others," Tracy volunteered. "The rest of you go over to the barn and fill all the buckets you can find outa that barrel of coal-oil."

"Let's get moving!" Grizzly Pete told the other outlaws. "We'll smoke that bastard Longarm outa them trees and when we git through using him for target practice he'll be dead'rn last year's Christmas turkey!"

Chapter 18

Hunkered down in the concealment of the pine grove, Longarm had listened while the outlaws were forming their plans. As the renegades started toward the barn, he turned his attention to Tracy, who stood with his back to Longarm's hiding place with his attention fixed on the men moving across the clearing toward the barn. Before he could rise from his crouch and move toward the outlaw, Longarm saw Fletcher approaching with the two men he'd been sent to bring back. He held his position and waited.

You better see what them fellows does, old son, he cautioned himself. *The odds you figured was with you ain't so good any more, but it's likely that Tracy's going to take them others along with him and go up to the barn to help the rest of them renegades, and maybe that'll even up the odds again.*

Within the next few moments, Longarm saw that he had guessed correctly. As soon as Fletcher and his companions were within easy hailing distance, he heard Tracy call to them.

"Slant up to the barn," he ordered the approaching trio, starting across the clearing himself. "The faster we get those buckets filled up with coal-oil up there, the quicker we'll get our hands on Longarm!"

When the four outlaws were well out of earshot, Longarm made his move. Dodging from tree to tree along the edge of the pines, he soon reached the nearest of the cabins that were nestled close to the trees. Using the little buildings to cover his movements, he timed his movements to the progress that Tracy and his group were making toward the barn. He reached the last cabin only a few moments after the outlaws had joined their fellows lined up at the coal-oil barrel.

Tracy and his trio of late arrivals stood a little way apart from the group that had gotten to the barrel first. Longarm stopped and peered around the rear wall of the cabin to watch the renegades at work.

Those who had reached the barn first had moved the barrel of coal-oil just outside the yawning doors and were crowding around it, dipping their buckets in to fill them with the inflammable liquid. As each one filled his pail, Tracy pointed to a spot in front of the big stand of pines where the outlaws thought Longarm was still hiding and waved them toward it.

Though Longarm had been watching for only a few minutes, he could see how Tracy's plan was supposed to work. It was obvious that he intended for all the men to move forward at the same time, wetting down the duff with coal-oil as they entered the pines. Then, as soon as the duff had been well soaked, the duff would be lighted in half a dozen places at once and they would stand back while the wind fanned the flames into a solid wall of fire that would sweep through the trees.

Finally the last of the improvised bucket brigade left. Tracy picked up one of the two or three remaining buckets, dipped it into the barrel, and brought it out full and dripping. He started after his fellows.

While the outlaws worked busily, filling their buckets, Longarm had watched silently. With the odds so heavily against him, he had known from the beginning that if he tried to capture the renegades as a group his chances for failure outweighed those for success. Now, even with his adversaries scattering, he saw that he was going to have his hands full trying to keep all of them covered.

You got to figure a way to get 'em scattered out, he told himself silently. *Then you can take one or two at a time, and maybe corral every last man of 'em before they know what's happened to 'em.*

Looking around for anything he could use to do the job he needed, his eyes reached the coal-oil barrel.

"That'll do it!" he exclaimed aloud. "It's sorta like throwing the baby out with the bathwater, but it's the best thing you got handy, so you might as well use it."

Glancing quickly across the clearing, he saw that the outlaws had spread out into a straggling, wide-spaced line at the edge of the pine growth and were moving toward the trees. The realization that he had virtually no time left spurred Longarm into action.

Running up to the barrel of coal-oil, he glanced into it and saw that the gang had left it almost half full. Placing his rifle on the ground, Longarm tilted the barrel and rolled it on its bottom edge into the barn. He lowered the barrel near the center of the cavernous building. Two empty pails stood just inside the door. Longarm grabbed one of them and dipped it into the barrel, then splashed the volatile liquid across the floor toward one wall.

With the penetrating smell of the raw coal-oil beginning to fill the air, Longarm splashed a second trail of coal-oil to the opposite wall. By now the air in the big barn was heavy with the fumes from the oil Longarm had spilled. He dipped his pail into the barrel to refill it once more, and let the eye-smarting liquid splash in a wide swathe behind him as he backed toward the yawning doors.

He stopped just outside, in the clear air, long enough to take a cigar from his pocket and clamp it between his teeth. Then he flicked an iron-hard thumbnail across the match-head, calmly lighting a cheroot. When it was drawing to his satisfaction he dropped the still-burning match into the oil-soaked straw at his feet.

For an instant the match flickered and almost died. Then it

ignited the straw. A line of blue flame flared, flickered, then flared again and came to life with an ominous crackle.

Longarm moved quickly. Taking long strides, he started for the door. He reached it in half a dozen steps, grabbed up his Winchester as he passed it, and kept going. He looked back once and saw three lines of yellow flame dancing along the floor, brightening the barn's interior. One line led to the coal-oil barrel from the point where Longarm had lighted his incendiary trail. Two other lines were sweeping away from the first, racing toward the barn's side walls.

From the corral Longarm heard the penned-up horses whinnying in shrill excitement. Racing to the corral gate, moving almost as fast as the lines of flame heading for the barn's walls, he flung the gates open and whistled loudly. One of the horses nearest him had not yet panicked too greatly to respond. It neighed loudly and dashed toward the gate. With one of their corral-mates to follow now, the other horses raced toward the open gate and streamed past Longarm, scattering as they bolted.

Suddenly a loud whooshing sound came from the barn, a noise like an enormous burst of wind racing ahead of a gale. As Longarm turned to look at the building, a pillar of oily smoke roiled from its gaping doors. The smoke was followed by a low-pitched roar. Then a massive tongue of flame shot through the smoke as the partly filled barrel of coal-oil ignited.

Loud shouts coming from the line of pines across the clearing reached Longarm's ears now above the roaring of the flames. He turned and looked toward the trees. The outlaws were racing toward the barn, yelling and waving their arms. The roar of the flames filling Longarm's ears reduced the shouts of the approaching men to garbled nonsense, but he had his plan firmly in mind and knew exactly what he had to do.

Dropping to the ground, Longarm flattened himself out and shouldered his rifle. He recognized Fletcher in the center of the ragged line of running outlaws, picked him as his first target, and triggered off two quick shots.

Longarm had aimed to wound, not to kill. Fletcher stum-

178

bled when the slug plowed into his thigh, then lurched forward and fell to the ground, where he lay still. Twistnose and Barclay had been flanking Fletcher on either side, and when they saw their fellow outlaw drop they broke the ragged line of their advance. Running to the fallen man, they bent over to help him.

Seeing the number of his attackers reduced momentarily by three, Longarm swung the Winchester's muzzle along the ragged line of moving men. He aimed at Scotty and fired again. Scotty stumbled, then moved ahead, limping. This time the men running beside the wounded outlaw did not stop, and Longarm triggered off a second shot at the nearest, Grizzly Pete. The man toppled and fell into a huddled heap on the ground.

Shots were sounding from the few remaining outlaws. They were well within pistol range now, and hot lead was cutting the air around Longarm. Most of the slugs whistled harmlessly past him, but two or three raised spurts of dirt uncomfortably close.

They ain't stopping to aim, he told himself. *But them damn outlaws is mostly pretty good shots and you're pushing your luck a mite too far.*

Parks and Smith, running almost side by side, were now the two outlaws nearest Longarm. He found Parks in the vee of the Winchester's sights and swung the Winchester's muzzle, gauging the running man's speed. Longarm swung the rifle barrel to give his moving target the necessary lead and fined his aim to take the outlaw in the thigh, shooting to wound, not to kill.

In the split second that lapsed while Longarm was squeezing off his shot he saw Parks bend forward, his face in the sights now instead of his legs. During that hair-thin slice of time, Longarm realized that Parks had seen he was a target and bent to avoid the bullet. It was too late to recall the shot. Longarm's lead sped true and the rifle slug drilled into the outlaw's skull.

Parks fell like he'd been poleaxed. With a wild shriek that shrilled above the cracks of gunshots from his fellow outlaws, Smith started running toward Parks's prone body. He held a

179

revolver in each hand and as he came closer he began firing in Longarm's general direction.

Out of habit, Longarm had been counting his shots. He realized when he triggered off the shot which brought Parks down that he'd emptied the Winchester's magazine. He dropped flat, fumbling in his pocket for cartridges, took them out, and began reloading. He glanced up when he heard Smith's screams, and saw that the outlaw had dropped both his pistols and was kneeling beside Parks's body.

When the booming of a shot broke through the keening cries rising from Smith's throat and the bullet plowed into the dirt a foot from his shoulder, Longarm glanced at the screaming outlaw. Smith was still on his knees beside Parks's body, but he'd picked up one of the revolvers that he'd dropped and was raising it in shaking hands to fire a second shot.

Longarm saw Smith's contorted face and quivering hands. He also saw that the range was too great for the outlaw to shoot accurately. Calmly, working by feel, he continued feeding shells into the Winchester's magazine, his fingers moving with the speed and precision born of long experience.

While he was working, Longarm had kept his eyes on Smith. When he saw the outlaw's hands stop shaking and raise one of his revolvers, Longarm was sliding the last cartridge into the Winchester's loading-port. He levered a shell into the chamber, took quick aim, and fired. The slug smashed into Smith's ribcage as the outlaw triggered his revolver. His hands went up and the bullet whistled harmlessly into the air.

Echoes of both Smith's and Longarm's shots were dying in the air when a rifle barked behind Longarm and the slug whistled past his ear. As he was turning his head to look for the man who'd apparently outflanked him, the rifle cracked again. This time the bullet lifted Longarm's hat off his head. The hat sailed a yard through the air and fell to the ground.

Even before his hat started falling to earth, Longarm was rolling over to bring his rifle to bear on the outlaw who was sniping at him from behind. What he saw almost froze his finger on the Winchester's trigger.

Fifty yards or so away, a ghostly white-shrouded figure was lurching unsteadily across the clearing. For a moment

180

Longarm thought he was looking at a phantom, and his finger froze on the trigger of his rifle. All the outlaws around the clearing had stopped shooting at the sight of the white-draped apparition. When the ghostly white form raised the rifle it carried, the spell was broken. Though Longarm had not noticed the weapon in his first surprised glance, he realized now that the ghostlike form was the outlaws' boss, wearing a long white nightshirt.

Longarm was turning, bringing up his Winchester as he moved, when he saw that the white-draped figure was beginning to sway unsteadily. The rifle drooped, then fell from its hands. The white-gowned man wrapped his arms around his abdomen. He stood swaying back and forth for a moment. Then, with a fading shriek of agony, his head dropped forward and his knees buckled and he crumpled slowly to the ground.

For the first time Longarm realized that the outlaws were no longer shooting. Only four of them were left: Grizzly Pete and Twistnose, Tracy and Barclay. Ignoring Longarm, they had dropped their rifles and were running toward the white huddle of motionless cloth where the man they called "boss" had fallen. All of them still wore their gunbelts, and Longarm kept his rifle ready as they passed him, but they did not even glance in his direction. Longarm followed them.

By the time he reached them, they had straightened out the huddled form and were kneeling around it. The boss was still alive. His bronzed face had paled to an unhealthy yellow and his eyes were closed, but his chest was still rising and falling spasmodically as he breathed. A huge bloodstain was spreading over the white fabric of the nightgown where it covered his abdomen.

A moment after Longarm stopped beside the little group of kneeling outlaws, the recumbent man's eyelids fluttered and opened. He glanced at the men close to him, then raised his eyes to look at Longarm.

"You are not Anders," he said. The words came slowly from his pale lips; his voice was feeble. "You are not one of us at all."

"No," Longarm said. "I sure ain't. My name's Long, deputy U. S. marshal outa the Denver office. Anders got killed down in Walsenberg and I taken his double-eagle. I don't guess I need to tell you that every man jack of you's under arrest."

"Not if you're the one they call Longarm," Grizzly Pete said. "But, hell, I'd sooner put in a spell behind bars than go up against you agin."

Longarm nodded and looked back at the outlaw leader. "You'd be Reyna, I imagine. Rattlesnake Reyna, that's the name I picked up down in Tascosa."

"*Sí.* And you have spoiled my beautiful plan." Reyna's face contorted with pain. Longarm could see his body shudder under the rumpled fabric of the nightgown.

"Looks that way. But why in hell didn't you stay in bed like the doc told you to?"

"I heard the shooting," Reyna replied. His body arched and his face twisted for a moment. Then the spasm passed and he went on, "But before then a great pain had awakened me and I knew that I must die." Another spasm twisted him and contorted his face. When he spoke again, he lapsed into his native tongue. His voice was feeble as he said, *"No es importante. La vida 'sta un chiste grande, no mas."*

Longarm pulled his favorite red morocco-upholstered chair up to Vail's paper-littered desk and laid his bullet-torn Stetson in front of the chief marshal.

"Looks like you owe me another hat, Billy," he said.

Vail stared at the abused Stetson for a moment, then told Longarm, "Maybe. Maybe not. I'll decide that after I see your report. Damn it, Long, where've you been? Judge Parker's been sending me a telegram every day wanting to know when you're going to bring back Gunge Peyton."

"Why, I can't bring Peyton back on account of I had to shoot him."

Longarm took a crumpled bandanna from his coat pocket and spread it out on Vail's desk. A little heap of square packets made of thin leather lay on the red cloth. He opened each of them in turn, took out the double-eagles they contained, and lined the gold pieces up neatly in front of Vail.

"While I was chasing down Gunge Peyton, I run across a

182

new gang of outlaws that was getting together. Them double-eagles is how they knew each other. But it's a long story, Billy, and a lot of them are dead, too. I'll write up my report and you can read what happened."

Vail stared at the coins for a moment, then raised his eyes to Longarm. "I suppose I owe you the hat, all right," he said. "Put in the voucher and I'll approve it. Oh, yes—I've got a telegram for you, too." He reached into his desk drawer and took out an envelope. "It just came in yesterday."

"I guess I better look at it," Longarm said, tearing the envelope open. He read the short message: *Business finally completed. Leaving San Francisco tomorrow. Will look for you at depot. Julia.*

Folding the message and stuffing it into his pocket, Longarm said, "I'd like to have that voucher for the hat right away, Billy. And I guess I got enough days off stacked up to not show up here for a day or so. You see, I got a little bit of important personal business that I need to tend to."

Watch for

LONGARM IN THE BIGHORN BASIN

one hundred and seventh novel in the bold
LONGARM series from Jove

coming in November!